The
Legend
of Garth

Larry Cochran

ISBN: 148014116X

ISBN-13: 9781480141162

"The Legend of Garth"

I am Angus the Elder.
Dragonslayer.

When I was young, my name struck fear in the hearts of dragons throughout the provinces. Now it lives only in the legends of the great green-scales. One hundred times one hundred dragons I met on the fields of valor, and one hundred times one hundred forfeited their heads to my sword, their hearts to my lance.

Now I am the Elder. When the soft hair grows on their chins, the young ones come to me. Wooden swords and padded lances give them the skills of the Dragonslayer. They run for miles, lift boulders and logs, and learn to walk on ropes to give them balance. When their beard is full, they leave with lances of yew and swords of steel to face the young blue and then the great green-scales on the field of valor.

I tell them of honor, and the glory of the Dragonslayer. When the sun rests and they are spent, they sit by my fire and hear the tales of glory.

I tell them of the glory of victory, advising to drink deep of the free ale, for in the morn they will be but a sunrise away from death.

I send them forth, the only sons I will ever know. For the Dragonslayer's lot is to live for battle, never knowing home or hearth.

Through the past fortnight, tales were told of an old one, a dragon with luminous turquoise scales and a tail the length of ten horses. Two dozen Dragon Slayers had joined him on the field of battle, and twenty four had not returned. Fear reigned in the provinces, and women despaired for their young.

Alone I saddled my steed, old but sure of foot and well-seasoned. I have no squire, so I donned my bright green armor alone. Taking my sword and lance from their places of honor, I rode to the field for a final taste of the Dragonslayer's lot.

As the sun rose over the heath, Garth stood with the sun to his back and the meadow to his fore. Slowly we moved to the center of the field. Slowly he bowed his head and touched one knee to the rye. Slowly, I placed the tip of my sword in the earth, bowing my head and kneeling.

I saw Garth slowly rise. The great one of the turquoise scales rose slowly from the rye, and I could see his pain. He watched as I used my sword to help me rise. With knowing nods, we separated.

The battle was joined.

Twice the sun crossed the sky as we battled. Twice we retired at sunset, spent beyond even our great experience.

On the morn of the third day, we again joined on the field. As the sun reached mid-day, my sword found a grip and Garth's head lay at my feet. My lance found his heart, laying the great one to his final rest.

The feast was great, but I drank lightly of the ale. The wenches were young and beautiful, but I turned them away one by one. At midnight, I joined the green scales in building a pyre for Garth the Great, and they granted me the honor of casting the torch that lit it ablaze.

The glory was mine, but the victory was Garth's. He knew, as did I, that the blue-scales would never turn green unless they vanquished great Dragonslayers. And there will never be great Dragonslayers until the scales turn green.

Garth knew our time has come and gone, and that the young ones need to take their places on the fields of valor. Garth gave himself to inspire the blue scales, and my young Dragonslayers.

Were it not so, I would have perished in the flames under the noon-day sun.

I am Angus the Elder. My sword stands in the field amid a pile of ash.

Long live the legend of Garth!

◆◆◆◆

Facing the Dragon

Chapter the First

Four young men stood before Angus the Elder, anxious to leave camp and make their name as a dragonslayers. It was up to Angus to prepare them for the voyage ahead.

"Lads," he began, "you have finished your training, and the time is nigh for you to venture forth and seek your fortune as Dragonslayers. But first, you must return to your father's house for the last time."

One by one, he handed them small purses of coins. Knowing what they contained, the young ones were prepared for the substantial weight of the small bags.

"Take these purses to your father's house, and present them to your mother. She will know what to do with them. These coins would take your father a lifetime to earn at honest labor. Your mother can spend them as she wishes, but all mothers save two coins for the memorial service which will inevitably come when you face a dragon that is faster, stronger, and more cunning than all your skills.

"Make peace with your father, for you will never again have the chance. Kiss your mother goodbye, for she will never again look on you as a son. The coins are small compensation for what they have sacrificed.

"You are straight and strong, and the maidens will seek you out. If you choose to bond with one, do not return to this camp. You are not yet a dragonslayer, and you can still become a father and husband if you wish. Many who trained here are constables, soldiers, or even farmers. You are stronger and more cunning than any man in your village, and you can be a great man if you choose to stay. There is no dishonor in deciding to live a simpler, more rewarding life. You owe me nothing.

"For, if you return, you will go to the battlefield and face the dragon. One of the combatants, either you or the dragon, will not emerge from the field of valor. It is the lot of the dragonslayer to face death over and over, knowing that today may be the day he will die in the flames. It is quite possible that while you are home you will decide not to die in such a manner. If so, Godspeed.

"I will be here when you return, if you return. We will go to the young ones, so that you and the dragons can take a full measure of each other. From there, we will travel to the central provinces, where you will face a blue scale in your first battle. If you survive, you will be a dragonslayer, and there is no turning back. You will live in legend, but you will never know the comfort of a wife or the joy of children.

"Weigh this decision well, for your decision is final."

Three of the four returned.

Stanford, Carlisle, and Wilson stood before Angus, holding the reins of their mounts. Three junior students served as squires. Three horses would accompany each of them. The novices would be mounted on the fastest, sturdiest mounts available, for they would ride them into battle. Squires were mounted on smaller horses, solid enough for a long ride. The pack horse would carry the armor, lance and sword, along with provisions for the trip.

It was sunrise when the company mounted and rode to the east.

At late afternoon, they came to the Great Channel. A ferry awaited them, and Angus paid a gold coin for the passage. Just after dark, they arrived on the western shore of the provinces.

Only a short ride later, the band made camp for the night. Squires unloaded and groomed the horses, while Angus and his students set the campfire.

As the journey progressed, they would find game and fresh water. For now, dry bread and jerky quelled their hunger, while ale quenched their thirst and relaxed their tired muscles. The fire was still blazing as the travelers fell asleep.

Breakfast was sourdough and fruit, washed down with warm water.

Day in and day out, the troop traveled toward the morning sun. They saw dragons, but the great ones paid no mind to the travelers. On the fourth day, they came upon a green scale basking in a meadow. The young ones turned to Angus, who motioned for them to wait.

Angus dismounted and walked onto the meadow. The boys were terrified, for Angus wore no sword and carried no lance as he ventured forth to face the dragon. As he approached, the dragon raised her head and snorted a small burst of fire.

Angus continued to approach.

Standing, the dragon faced Angus. Even boys who had never seen a dragon could see the curiosity in the dragon's face.

Angus stopped, well within the range of the dragon's fire.

"You are Angus," the dragon said, "slayer of Garth."

"That I am," came the reply.

"You honor me with your presence." The boys watched as the dragon appeared to smile.

"I regret disturbing you from your nap," Angus replied. "We will be crossing this meadow, and I did not wish to startle you."

Even the squires could see the smile on the dragon's face.

"Seeing you is never a disturbance" came the reply. "Are you headed to the land of the rising sun?"

"Aye," Angus replied. "There will be three new men seeking to be dragonslayers," he agreed, much to the despair of his students.

"Then we will meet again at the great meadow," replied the dragon, nodding. "I look forward to it."

"As do I," Angus replied, bowing.

When the troop reached him, Angus mounted his horse and made a path around the head of the dragon. The others barely breathed as they passed within reach of the great dragon's head.

"Farewell, old one. I will see you in the meadow," Angus cried as the last horse passed the dragon's head.

"Farewell, Angus, slayer of Garth," the dragon replied, raising her head and looking at the retreating group.

The sun rose and set many times as the troop continued on their journey. One small deer and dozens of rabbits replaced the jerky for their evening meals. They encountered no more sleeping dragons as they ventured on, and Angus rode around the few villages they found along the way.

Late one afternoon, they approached a meadow. The sun was low, but Stanford quickly picked out the reflection of a bright object in the center of the glade.

"Sir!" he called out to Angus. "What is shining in the meadow?"

Angus smiled. "It is a sword, standing where it was plunged into the earth."

Stanford smiled excitedly. "Your sword, sir?"

"Yes," Angus replied. "It is the sword used to slay Garth."

The boys seemed spellbound as the rode forward toward the sword. When they had reached the large pile of ashes surrounding it, they stopped. For many minutes, the stared at it, memorizing the lines and letters of the most famous sword in all the world.

Having given time to admire the weapon, Angus turned his horse to the east. One by one, the others followed.

By the fire that evening, Stanford was the one to ask what was on everyone's mind.

"Sir," he said tentatively. "Why did you leave the sword in the meadow, and why has no one taken it from there?"

Angus thought for a while before answering.

"The sword stands where it is because that is my way of honoring Garth the Great, the fiercest, most cunning, and deadliest dragon ever. That sword will remain there until another dragon as great as Garth is vanquished on that field." Smiling to himself, Angus added, "I doubt it will ever be claimed."

The boys nodded at each other. They had heard the legend, but seeing the sword made it more real to them than the stories by the campfires.

"I have heard that his scales were turquoise," Stanford ventured.

"Yes," Angus replied. "And they shone even when there was no sun, no torches, and no firelight. They had a light of their own, as only the greatest dragons may display."

"How many dragon slayers fell to Garth?" Stanford asked.

"No one knows," came the reply. "Dragons take courage and cunning from the dragonslayers they conquer," he explained, "just as dragonslayers take magic from vanquished dragons. Baby yellow scales grow naturally into blue scales, just as you grew a beard and hardened your muscles. Each time a dragon fights and wins, his scales become darker and greener. Only one dragon has ever had the turquoise scales, and it took the lives of thousands of dragon-slayers to give Garth his color."

That night, the boys barely slept as each one dreamed of becoming the dragonslayer who could claim the famous sword.

The sun rose and set many times as they ventured eastward. One morning Angus gathered them before telling them to mount.

"We are in the high country," he told them, "where yellow scales move about. Do not unsheathe your sword before a yellow scale; if you do, you will die quickly in its mother's fire. You are here to observe them and gain respect for the size and agility of your adversary. Study them well, for you will soon meet their older brothers and sisters on the field of battle."

"Sir," Wilson ventured, "What would happen if a yellow scale were to burn one of us in its fire?"

Angus smiled. "I would slay it," he replied, "but that would be small consolation if you were the one that got burned."

The boys were silent as they rode forward.

Almost immediately, they spotted a yellow tail being pushed from a rock by its mother. There was much flapping of wings until, moments before hitting the hard earth, the baby stopped its fall and hovered. Even the boys could see the young one's surprise and pride in its first flight.

Through the day they saw others, and came close to many. Angus watched the boys' faces as they first realized that even young dragons had necks longer than the boys were tall. One young dragon took a deep breath, intending to scorch the small troop, but its mother grabbed it by the tail and flew away before it could do harm.

All went as planned until late afternoon, when a great green landed in front of the band as they approached a rocky knoll. She faced them, shooting smoke from her nose.

Angus stopped, as did his students. He watched the strange behavior of the green scale, wondering why she would confront them this way.

Slowly, Carlisle dismounted and walked toward the dragon.

The dragon cried loudly as Carlisle approached. Angus nodded approvingly as Carlisle kept his sword in its scabbard and bowed to the great beast. Nodding her head toward him, she cried out again. All but Angus and Carlisle covered their ears as the deafening cry blew past them.

"She has lost her yellow scale," Angus told him. "And for some reason cannot take him back."

Carlisle never took his eyes off the dragon. Quietly, he asked her, "Can you show me where he is?"

The dragon turned, bringing her tail within inches of knocking Carlisle over. Without flinching, he held his ground, trusting her not to strike him. When she moved toward an opening in the rocks, Carlisle followed her. Angus motioned for the others to stay where they were, then followed well behind Carlisle, letting him deal with the dragon on his own terms.

The opening in the rocks was too small for even the head of the great green. While she stood at the opening, Carlisle moved ahead and entered.

"Sword, boy!" Angus called out behind him. Without slowing, Carlisle drew his sword and moved forward.

The smell of the cave was nauseating, but Carlisle moved ahead, sword at ready. Inside, he could hear the snarling of some type of beast and the cries of the young dragon.

The entrance opened to a large room. As his eyes adjusted, the first things Carlisle could see were the eyes of the beasts, snarling and circling the yellow scale.

"Lycans!" Carlisle thought. He had never seen them, but he had heard the tales of the beasts that walked and thought like a man, but had the body of a wolf. They must have herded the young one in here where its mother could not protect it. No doubt they had an exit somewhere that would allow them to escape the wrath of its parents.

The man-wolves found him at the same time he saw them. Leaving the young dragon, they pressed forward towards him.

Carlisle felt the explosion of fear, but he took comfort in the weight and balance of the weapon in his hand. As the first lycan leaped forward for the kill, its head hit the floor a good two feet from its body.

First blood!

As the others ran to him, Carlisle could hear the singing of his sword as it swung back and forth, to and fro. Instincts born from long hours of training let his sword do its work while his eyes searched for the next attacker.

Almost as fast as it started, it was over. Over a dozen dead lycans lay at Carlisle's feet, and his sword was covered in blood.

Slowly, he circled the young dragon, preparing to herd it back to its mother.

Suddenly he felt movement behind him. Before he could turn, he felt the lycan leap in his direction. His sword was out, but he heard a yelp and felt the lycan pass him on its way to the floor of the cave. Looking at it, he could see the shiny hilt of a long knife protruding behind its right foreleg.

As he stared at the dead beast, his teacher passed him silently. Before Carlisle even realized there was movement, Angus was retrieving his knife.

"I'll let a dragon take you, if that's your fate," Angus said briskly, "but not the likes of this one."

The yellow scale needed no herding as it ran past the men and out to its mother.

Angus and Carlisle walked together, blinking as they entered the bright sunlight.

The dragon turned to Carlisle, giving him a half-bow by bending one knee and lowering her head.

As he returned the gesture, her great tongue reached out and surrounded him. It was as wet as a soaked sponge, and she literally rolled him up in it and then let it unroll, leaving him standing but drenched.

Carlisle didn't know what to say or do, so he stood there.

The green scale, and her baby, turned and flew away.

Carlisle stood, soaked from head to toe by dragon spit. Angus was laughing, which caused the young man to blush.

"Damn!" The word burst from Carlisle suddenly and with substantial force. He was shaking his hands and head, casting off the water like a wet dog.

Angus laughed even harder.

Looking to his teacher, he asked, "Why did she do THAT?"

Angus regained his composure.

"You were covered in lycan blood, and probably have a scratch or two. If you don't remove it, you would soon be one of them." Angus motioned toward the cave. "She bathed you, and the magic in her spittle will heal your wounds and destroy the infectious blood."

Carlisle shook his head and walked toward his companions.

By the fire that evening, Angus watched Carlisle tell the tale of saving the yellow scale from a band of lycans. In the story, there were more lycans and they were bigger than Angus remembered, but the lad told a compelling tale of his heroics.

Angus smiled. There was hope that this one would be a great dragonslayer. If not, some dragon was going to get a lot more courage and cunning than he deserved from such a young adversary.

◆◆◆

The Expatriation of Angus

Chapter the Second

Evening fell as the troop reached the meadow of the sword. They had been riding for several days, and the anticipation of facing a dragon weighed heavily on each potential dragonslayer. Angus started the camp fire while the squires curried the horses and set the camp. The would-be dragonslayers were sent by Angus to run laps around the meadow carrying logs; this was as much for their morale and to help them sleep as it was for their fitness.

One of the squires trapped a dozen hares, which were a welcome break from the jerky and venison they had been living on. Another squire found a small garden and foraged enough carrots, potatoes and onions to make a fine stew. The contributor of the vegetables ate last, since Angus sent him to find the owner of the garden and pay him five pence (a princely sum) for the appropriated vegetables.

The fire was still bright as they finished their meal, and Wilson asked Angus to tell them about his exile to the "other earth". Drawing deep on his pipe, he began to tell the tale.

After vanquishing Garth, Angus had felt younger and more fit than he had in a very long time. He was as strong, fast and cunning as any man with half his battles. While he deeply mourned the loss of Garth, Angus considered becoming active again as a dragonslayer. He knew it was Garth's magic that made him feel that way, but he was fine with enjoying the new-found youth while it lasted.

Angus had ordered a new broadsword to replace the one he had left in the field of ashes. Carefully he supervised its composition, annoying the dwarf who oversaw the careful fusing of the nickel and iron, along with the secret crystal ores, in exactly the right proportions. Only the elder dwarfs, many of whom remembered more summers than even Angus, could forge the special steel, and they would do the work only for the dragonslayers. When the steel was ready, it was folded one hundred times to make the blade as strong and flexible as possible, as well as shiny and sharp.

Each dragonslayer had a sword balanced and fitted to his hand. While all the swords looked the same from afar, each was exactly three times the length of the owner's forearm and weighted according to its owner's constitution. Along each blade, save this one, was the name and genealogy of its owner, written in Elven script. This new sword bore only the legend, "Angus, Slayer of Garth".

It was a fit sword, and a fit legend.

Angus engaged a squire, suitable for an active dragonslayer. His old steed was still able and strong, and his lance required only a good polishing to be ready for battle. Once all the arrangements were made, Angus traveled to the middle provinces, camping on the edge of the great meadow where his old sword stood in testament to the greatest battle every joined.

Mornings came and evenings went. No great green scales arrived to join him in battle. Angus became impatient, and rode around the great meadow, looking for other dragonslayers. None were present, and none arrived.

Finally, as Angus slept, the sorcerer Garand appeared to him as a dream.

"Angus," spoke the great Garand. Although it was custom for Angus to be addressed formally as "the Elder", Garand had been ancient when Angus was just a lad.

"Aye, Garand," Angus dreamed. "What brings you to the field of battle?"

"It is a lonely meadow now," mused Garand. "The great Garth is gone, and no green scale wishes to battle the great Angus, Slayer of Garth. Dragonslayers remain elsewhere, with no dragons to battle." The specter of Garand shook his head. "We have lost the balance, and the world cannot continue as it was."

"Where are the dragons, and the dragonslayers, Great One?" Angus asked. "Perhaps I can rouse them to battle."

"No," Garand replied, shaking his head. "Your magic is too great, and none will challenge you. While you remain, no dragon will arrive. As long as you are here, no dragonslayer will appear to challenge a dragon, for you are their venerated elder."

Angus was sorely troubled by this observation from Garand. "Then how will the blue scales earn their green, and how will dragonslayers gain in strength and magic?"

"They cannot, so long as you remain." The wizard's image leaned forward, raising his finger to the ancient dragonslayer. "You must leave until the balance is restored. You must go where no dragons fly, and where the dragonslayers cannot wait for you to save them."

Angus shook his head sadly. "Where would that be?" he asked the sorcerer.

As quickly as he thought the question, Angus could see a strange world of buildings, built of a single stone, towering to the heavens. All manner of people moved about, dressed strangely and not even acknowledging the passing of others. The air was foul, but not from the stench of rotting food and animals; it had a strange bitter smell unlike any Angus had encountered.

"It is the other Earth," Garand explained. "The one of legend, where time and distance rule the day. It is a place where you can go with your magic and not be detected by any."

Suddenly the buildings and people were gone, but Angus could see himself. He was dressed strangely, clothes made of cloth smoother than any worn by the women of his world, and brightly colored. Angus' hair was groomed and his beard shorn, but it was him.

"How am I to survive in this strange land?" he asked. "I have never seen such a place, and I will be alone without my lance."

"You will be as you are, but your magic can make you appear familiar to the people in this place," Garand explained. "They worship science, not magic, so you will be able to move about undetected and obtain the provisions and lodging you need. You will learn to walk with them, and remain there until the balance has been restored to our lands. Then you can return, as the Elder, but you must never again take the field as a dragonslayer."

Angus knew he was bound to do as the sorcerer suggested, for he too had felt the strange imbalance since his battle with Garth. He had ignored it, pushed it away, by becoming busy in the preparation for battles he had always known would not come. The time for denial had passed, and it was time to do what needed to be done to preserve the balance between dragons and men.

"Go to the eastern provinces," Garand commanded. "There you will find a yellow scale, last daughter of Garth. She is also strong with magic, and she can accompany you in your exile."

As quickly as it began, the dream of Garand vanished and Angus returned to his rest.

In the morning, he saddled his horse and sent his squire home, carrying the lance and armor Angus had dreamed of using in battle. They would be returned to their place of honor, never again to be called forth in glory.

Traveling eastward, he sought the daughter of Garth.

The journey was uneventful, and Angus had no trouble locating the daughter of Garth. Her mother was a giant green scale, following her daughter around the nesting grounds. Garth paid his respects to her mother, and then explained the directions he received from Garand. She, too, had been visited by visions of Garand, and sadly accepted the need for her daughter to go with the Elder in his exile.

Garth's daughter, Erin, was thrilled to join him in their quest. Long ago, her scales should have turned blue. She sensed that things were not as they should be, and greeted a chance to make things right with the enthusiasm only the very young can know.

Angus and Erin traveled westward, bidding her mother farewell. Neither knew their destination, but they trusted Garand to guide them. Passing through unfamiliar mountains, they saw the great city from Angus' dream. Walking westward toward the city, he expected a flash of light, or roll of thunder, or shimmering portal to mark their transformation. Instead, one moment he was Angus the Elder, walking with a dragon. The next moment, he was neatly groomed and walking with a small dog.

Magic can be truly a wondrous thing, he thought.

He hated the bitter stench of the city, but Erin seemed right at home. Angus wondered if the caves of the dragons had that smell; a bitter, smoky smell from burning rocks and the black water that seeped from the rocks of the breeding grounds.

As they passed through the city streets, Angus walked slowly, observing all the new sights, sounds and smells. Erin pranced about as if she had been a dog all her life. Clearly, she was adjusting to this new world better than Angus.

A young boy emerged from the stone path south of the building where Angus and Erin were approaching from the east.

"Boy," he called out. The youngster stopped. "Where can we find lodging?"

The boy looked at him with annoyance, then curiosity. As he studied Angus, the anger faded from his face and courage replaced it.

"You want a hotel, or a house?" the boy asked.

"A room, for now," Angus ventured, not knowing what a hotel might be.

"How long you staying?" asked the boy in a businesslike tone.

"I am not sure," answered Angus, "but it will be many days."

"My mom is the manager at an apartment complex," the boy offered. "But you will have to pay a deposit if you want to keep your dog there."

Angus reached into his pocket and removed the purse where he carried gold coins. It was light, weighing almost nothing. Looking inside, he found only bits of paper.

"How much will I need?" Angus asked the young innkeeper. As he took the roll of paper from his purse, the young man became excited.

"Man, put that wad away!" he said quickly, looking about as if he expected trouble from all sides.

"But, I'm not sure how much I have or will need," Angus explained. "Can you assist me?"

"Yeah," the boy said quietly, "but keep it down low and out of sight." Quickly he approached Angus, reaching for the scraps of paper.

The boy flipped through the paper and separated several scraps from the others. Handing back the remainder of the roll, he instructed, "Put this back in the bag." Angus returned the paper to his purse. "Now," said the boy, handing back to scraps he had retained, "put this in your pocket. It's enough for first and last month's rent, plus the animal deposit."

Angus did as instructed. In his world, no boy would have dared speak to him this way, but he sensed goodness in the actions of the boy and determined not to let the informality of the boy's bearing disturb him. Erin also sensed the boy's honor and was rubbing against his leg, encouraging him to scratch her behind her ears.

"Where the Hell are you from?" the boy asked as he led them away.

"The east," Angus replied.

"Well, around here you had better keep that roll out of sight, or you will find yourself on the wrong end of a knife," the boy warned.

Angus smiled. So there were highwaymen in this world as well. He had never feared them before, since no highwayman would ever dare attack a dragonslayer. But this was a new world, and he would remain prepared for new adventures.

The young man's mother was happy to take his scraps of paper in exchange for a room, and the boy had counted out exactly the number of scraps she demanded. Angus simply pulled them from his pocket and handed them to her. She was surprised, but pleased as she counted the papers.

When the exchange was done, Angus let the lad speak for him, since he clearly knew the appropriate time for their stay and how to explain it. The mother handed the boy something shiny, and he led Angus and Erin down a series of tunnels with doors on one side. Near the end of the second tunnel, they climbed stairs leading to another series of tunnels. Angus noted the path, remembering the number of steps and the number of turns so he could make the return journey. Suddenly, the boy stopped before a door and stabbed the shiny object into a ball protruding from its surface.

By the standards of his world, this room was enormous. Angus was amazed that there were even more rooms than the one he had entered. There was a room where someone could prepare a meal, a room with an elevated palate to sleep on, and a room with strange white seats and bowls.

Getting used to this world might be a little more difficult than Angus expected.

The boy had apparently finished giving Angus a tour of his new house. As they walked together into the main room, the boy stopped suddenly. He was looking at a shiny window which seemed to look back into the room, rather than outside. Angus had noticed it when they arrived, but now the boy was staring into it as if he had seen a ghost.

Looking at the window, Angus saw his reflection and that of Erin. In the reflection, he was not neatly groomed and dressed in bright clothes; instead, he saw only the course cloth, sword, leather belt, and long knife he had been wearing when he began his journey. And, standing next to him, he saw a yellow scale.

"Holy shit!" exclaimed the boy. "You're the Dragonslayer!"

••••

Living in the New Land

Chapter the Third

ngus had long ago decided that there was nothing left that could take him off guard, but he had been wrong. As the boy nearly shook with excitement, Angus was at a total loss about how to respond to being recognized.

Finally, he spoke. "How do you know me, boy?" he boomed.

The boy's excitement seemed to dissipate, then returned in a calmer form.

"First," replied the boy, "calling anyone a "boy" will start a fight you don't really want. In this world, if you don't know someone's name call them "Dude" or "Man", but not "boy." The young man looked again at Angus, then into the reflective window, then back at Angus and Erin. "Looking like that..." he said thoughtfully, "if you don't know someone's name call the men "Sir" and the women "Ma'am"; that'll do it." Pausing momentarily, he seemed satisfied with his instructions.

"My name's Andrew," he said matter-of-factly, holding out his hand in the universal position of one who wanted to shake hands.

In his world, Angus would never shake hands with a mere lad; most of them were afraid of him, and the few who weren't were hardly worth socializing with. Instinctively, though, Angus took the proffered hand and shook it strongly. The lad had a strong grip, he noticed approvingly.

"Angus, "he stated simply, shaking vigorously. Having finished the handshake, Angus thought about what the lad and told him, taking this bit of etiquette to heart. "Sir or ma'am it shall be!"

"As to recognizing you, I play Dragon's Tale XD all the time. You and Erin, there, are key players." Seeing that Angus did not understand his answer, Andrew simply said, "Wait here," and ran out the door.

Within minutes, Andrew returned and began stabbing tiny daggers, connected to strings, into the strange black window in the center of the main room's wall.

As Andrew moved away, the black window suddenly came to life with a view quite unfamiliar to Angus. There was a man, resembling him as he was in his own world. At the top of the screen were the words, "Dragon's Tale XD". Strangely, his image seemed to be jumping and running, slashing the sword back and forth, lopping off the heads of one strangely passive dragon after another. Having lopped off one dragon's head, his image was running away before the dragon's magic had been received, only to lop off another dragon's head in the same bizarre manner.

Before Angus could ask about the strange image and its peculiar behavior, the image changed to one of him standing next to a variety of words. They did not seem, to Angus, to even be related to one another, let alone make up a sentence. They said, "New Game", "Continue", and "Options". As Andrew pushed and pulled on the little black box he held in both hands, Angus' sword pointed to "continue" and the image again changed.

The next image said, "Load Game" at the top. Below those words was a list of several peculiar names. The list included "Andrew", "Bodacious", "Nuadelenn", "Melah", and "Melahnav". Angus' sword pointed to Andrew's name, and the image blinked before being replaced by a new one.

Angus continued to stare at the strange image that appeared in the window.

"This is my Dragon's Tale XD game," he reported proudly. "I played this every day after I came home, and some of my friends play with me. It's an RPG—Role Playing Game—so you can pick who you want to be. Sometimes I am the dragon, sometimes I am the dragonslayer, but it is always fun to play."

Seeing that Angus did not comprehend what he was telling him, Andrew waited a few seconds, watching Angus' face as he looked at the game screen.

"Anyway," he ventured, "that's you. You're Angus the Elder, Slayer of Garth, the greatest dragonslayer of all time."

Angus nodded, knowing Andrew spoke the truth, but not understanding at all how he could know such a thing.

"Weird, though," Andrew mused. Angus was about to agree with him when he continued, "about a week ago all the games locked up. Not just mine, but everyone's—worldwide. Couldn't get the dragons to fight, nor the dragonslayers. No one could even get them together on screen, let alone into a battle.

"The manufacturer posted a patch on the internet. I downloaded it, but I can no longer play as you—I can be anyone else, dragon or dragonslayer, but it is as if you have vanished.

"Now I can fight again, but it can't be as Angus."

Angus had no idea what Andrew was talking about, but it some-how seemed to be related to his quest in this strange world.

Looking away from the magic window, he gazed again at the re-flective one that showed him as he had been in his world, rather than as he wished to appear in this one. His reflection, and that of Erin, needed to be of this world, rather than their own. As he pon-dered, he looked at Erin and wondered if she could make the reflec-tions match their current appearance.

When he looked back at the reflective window, his image was exactly as he wished. He stood, dressed in bright clothes with a trimmed beard, while a small dog danced at his feet. Erin was clearly proud of herself for this finishing touch of magic, and Angus found himself bending to scratch behind her ears. It was a truly alien ges-ture, since he would never have petted a dog in his real world, and since he knew she was no dog at all, but a dragon with bright yellow scales.

Andrew noticed the change immediately.

"How'd she do that?" he asked incredulously.

"Dragons are magic," Angus replied absently.

"Well," Andrew responded cautiously, "she'd better keep it that way. You can kick ass in the game, but some of the folks around here would love to get their hands on the real Angus. I'm not sure what they'd do, but I'm sure they would have you tied up in a basement before you could count to three!"

Angus had no idea what a basement was, nor why he would be counting, but he left those facts for future reflection. Instead, he ac-cepted the warning from young Andrew as a caution well taken in this strange world.

Andrew began moving the strangely shaped black box, moving his fingers rapidly along the various buttons and the strange stick protruding from its face. As he moved his hands, the characters in the window seemed to move about. After a somewhat clumsy but interesting battle, a dragon's head lay before the dragonslayer in the window. Without waiting to receive magic, and without piercing the dragon's heart with his lance, the dragonslayer moved on to the next dragon.

Pondering these actions, Angus decided the person in the window was not a dragonslayer, but a common man pretending to be a dragonslayer. Resolving to end such a travesty, he asked Andrew, "How do I speak with the man in the window?"

Andrew looked confused, but looked carefully as Angus pointed to the television.

"That's a TV, or a monitor," he ventured, "and I'm making that man move. Why?"

"To leave a dragon on the field of battle without piercing his heart is cruel," he explained. "And leaving without taking his magic is disrespectful and crude. If you can somehow control this man, then he MUST take the magic by lancing the dragon in the heart."

"Well," Andrew replied thoughtfully, "I can get a lance, no problem. If it's that important to you."

Angus nodded. "Aye," he said. "It is essential."

Angus watched as the window returned to the scene in the beginning, and his own image quickly thrust the sword into "New Game". The window went dark, and then several panels appeared with pictures of dragonslayers and dragons on them. Angus' image stabbed the dragonslayer image, and a line was drawn across the screen. Before Angus' eyes could focus on the line, letters spelling "Melah" suddenly appeared as if someone had written them. One blink later and he could see a dragonslayer, wearing dull blue armor, standing before a meadow. The dragonslayer's hair was black and curly, like Andrew's, but Angus did not recognize him.

A dragon roared onto the field of battle. It was a green scale.

The dragonslayer raised his sword. "Stop!" shouted Angus.

Andrew looked up, confused. "This is the part where I slay the dragon," he said, matter-of-factly.

"No," Angus said sternly. "You must not. That be a green scale, and your armor is not even bright blue yet."

"And..." Andrew inquired.

"See," Angus replied, pointing to the window, or screen, or monitor, or whatever it was called.

The dragon had stopped, standing silently before the dragonslayer.

"If you can control the man," Angus said quietly, "Put the tip of his sword in the ground."

Andrew did as he was told, commenting, "Seems like a good way to get eaten."

"Now bow his head," Angus instructed.

Andrew did as told.

The dragon lowered its head slightly, bending its knees in a shallow bow.

The green scale withdrew, and Angus instructed, "Now, lad, draw your sword."

Andrew moved his hands and the sword turned upward in the ready position.

A blue scale appeared from off-screen, stopping before the dragonslayer. Without waiting, it lowered its head and bent its knees, waiting.

This time, Angus said, "Pull the man's sword to his helmet and make him kneel."

Andrews hands moved, but his eyes watched the screen.

The blue scale drew back, and Angus said, "Swing your sword, lad, and go to the ready. The battle is about to be joined."

As the blue scale reappeared, flying in from the top right of the screen, Andrews fingers moved quickly with a practiced precision. Strike, parry, thrust, strike, feint...Angus was impressed at the lad's skill and courage, even as the dragon struck again and again. In his excitement, Angus forgot himself.

"Slow down, lad!" he whispered. "You are spending your power by striking too early. If you want his head, wait until the last second and then strike as you move away."

Andrew did as told. Waiting until the dragon's flame was nearly on him, he stepped to the right and swung the sword as hard as he could. The dragon's head lay on the ground before him.

Andrew started his touchdown dance. Angus lay a hand on his shoulder.

"Nay, lad," he advised. "Get your lance and finish the job."

Andrews seemed irritated, but he did as told. Quickly, his fingers moved across the control box, putting the sword in its scabbard and picking up the lance. It seemed almost cruel as he pushed the lance into the dead dragon's forequarter.

Suddenly, the lance lit up as if it had been struck by lightning.

Andrew did not move the keys, but the dragonslayer drew his sword and held it, using both hands, as high as he could reach. The entire page lit up, but the light of the dragonslayer was nearly blinding. Instinctively, Andrew looked away for a couple of seconds.

When Andrew looked back at the screen, the dragonslayer was on his knees and the sword rested on the ground before him. Without knowing how he knew, Andrew realized that the dragonslayer was completely spent, and that his armor was now a slightly brighter blue.

Angus smiled.

"Good fight, lad," he said proudly. "You live to fight another day."

Andrew remained on his knees, jaw agape. He had always loved Dragon's Tale, but he had never known it could be like this. And he was so tired he was nearly falling asleep sitting in front of the TV.

After a few moments, Andrew told Angus good night and left for his own quarters.

Angus smiled. Strange world, indeed, but the lad showed promise. And Angus was almost as good at recognizing talent as he was at slaying dragons.

◆◆◆◆

The Training Begins

Chapter the Fourth

For several days, Andrew did not play Dragon's Tale. Angus waited for him to return from school, and then urged him to leave the apartment complex and take him around this strange village. After walking an hour or so, they would stop in a park and Angus would exercise, encouraging Andrew to join him.

Andrew was amazed that he could not keep up with the ancient dragonslayer. He was one of the fastest kids at school and had always found the exercises in gym to be more fun than challenge. On the first day, he did sixty pushups with the old man , then watched Angus as he did another forty. Sit ups turned out the same; Andrew gave out long before the old man finished. Finally they ran, and when Andrew could run no more Angus stopped, barely winded. Erin ran alongside them and seemed to fatigue even less than Angus.

After a week of diversions and exercise, Angus encouraged Andrew to play Dragon's Tale again. Again, a green scale approached first, and Andrew bowed to the beautiful beast. Again, the dragon withdrew and a blue scale appeared. This time, the battle lasted much longer and Andrew had reached the end of his endurance before the blue scale left him an opening. Stepping aside as he swung his sword, Andrew bested his new adversary. Again, he placed his sword in its scabbard and pierced the dragon's heart with his lance.

The light was even brighter than before, and Andrew literally fell asleep where he sat in front of the monitor. Angus woke him gently as the sun was setting, and Andrew went home and directly to bed.

Another week of exercise, and another blue scale. Andrew was again totally spent when he headed home.

When Andrew arrived home, his mother called him into the kitchen. When she gestured at a chair, he knew he was in trouble.

"Have you been upstairs again?" she asked.

"Yes," he said. He knew to keep his answers short and straight until she let him in on what she was thinking.

His mother shook her head. "I'm glad you're having a good time, but you need to keep your distance. It's not healthy for a young man to spend this much time with some old man."

Andrew smiled. "He's like a grandfather, really," he mused. "He's always encouraging me to do more, do better, pay attention more... in fact," he added, "he sounds a little like you."

His mother laughed at his final comment. After only a moment, though, her smile faded and she again looked concerned.

"You know he goes to the park every day while you're at school," she ventured tentatively.

"No," Andrew replied honestly. "What does he do there?"

"I was there the other day with Latisha. He runs the jogging trail—it's almost three miles long, you know—over and over. I stayed just to see how long he'd keep running. And I mean running—not jogging. He ran for over an hour, and only stopped when the senior citizens group started to do Tai Chi. He walked over and joined them, not even breathing hard from his run."

Andrew smiled. "I know," he said proudly. "He outruns me, does more pushups, and just kicks ass." Realizing he had sworn in front of his mother, he looked down and waited for her reproof. Instead, she gave him the "don't do that again, young man!" look. Again, the smile faded and she became quiet and serious.

"Andrew," she said quietly. "I know you like him. But I want you to keep your distance and please, please find some boys your age to play with. He may be nice," she said with finality, "but you are a young man and you need some friends besides some old guy who lives upstairs!"

"OK," Andrew agreed, reluctantly. "I'll cut back. But can I still play Dragon's Tale up there?"

"OK," his mother agreed, closing the negotiations. "Twice a week, and that's IT!"

"All right," Andrew said dejectedly. For a moment, he toyed with how he could work around the agreement, and then remembered his mother's wrath when she had caught him in the past. He decided to wait until report cards came out, then he'd renegotiate. His grades had been steadily climbing, and he was expecting the first all "A" report card ever. That would give him the leverage he needed to increase his time with Angus.

In their own room, Angus and Erin slept peacefully on the floor, unaware of the negotiations below.

The next morning, Angus and Erin went for their morning run. He ran for an hour along the concrete path that led from his building to what appeared to be the center of the city. He still felt awkward in his new attire, but he had to concede that the running suit and shoes Andrew had helped him pick out was much more comfortable than his heavy clothes and leather boots. The heat in this town was insufferable; the one advantage to his new life was something called air conditioning, which kept his quarters quite comfortable even on the hottest day.

The second leg of his run took him to the place Andrew called "the park". It was a lovely glade where couples and families gathered for quiet enjoyment. During the day, it was a gathering place for people who appeared quite a lot older than Angus, although his senses told him they had, in fact, seen far fewer summers than he. On certain days he saw Andrew's mother with a small girl who seemed to be related to her, but Angus did not perceive that it was her child. Perhaps a niece, he thought. That felt right, and Angus had learned to trust his feelings on such matters.

As he entered the park, he slowed to a walk and looked around. There was Andrew's mother and the child. Angus smiled; the woman was swinging the child, who was clearly having a wonderful time. He had noticed that Andrew's mother, unlike many of the other parents, did not leave the girl to her own entertainment. Instead, she was constantly swinging or otherwise assisting the girl in her play. Angus and Erin both enjoyed watching her whenever their paths crossed.

As Angus watched, something began to bother him. He perceived a mild sense of danger, and Erin was perking up as well, looking for the source of this premonition. He saw a group of young men, wearing the baggy trousers and strange headgear that was so common in this village. Today they had a strange glow of malice about them, and Angus stepped out to close the distance between himself and Andrew's mother. He barely noticed Erin following along, or the serious pace of her walk.

He approached Andrew's mother, making sure she saw and recognized him before he got too close. Erin ran to the child, who clearly loved to pet, pull, and pick up puppies.

"Good morning," he said cheerfully.

"Good morning," she responded. "Angus, isn't it?"

"Yes, Ma'am," he answered politely.

"Cherise," she said, holding out a delicate hand.

Angus bowed his head and accepted her hand. He felt a strange urge to kiss it, for she carried herself as if she were royalty. After a brief pause, he decided against it and felt her withdraw her hand.

"It is a pleasure to see you in such a lovely glade," Angus ventured.

"It is a beautiful day," Cherise responded. Curiosity showed on her face, and she asked, "Angus is quite an interesting name. Are you by chance British?"

Not knowing what British might be, Angus chose an obscure answer and hoped it would quell her curiosity. "I am from the Isles," he said, "but I've spent some time on the Continent. Right now, I'm happy to be a visitor in this beautiful land."

Cherise smiled. She was so totally charmed by the man that she did not sense the young men approaching from her rear.

"Hey, Mama," one young man said loudly. "Leave that old fart alone and come get some of a real man." He grabbed his crotch obscenely, and the other men laughed.

Angus saw Cherise's face cloud with anger, but she move closer to the child and kept her tongue. Erin moved between the child and the men. The child was so busy petting Erin that she didn't even notice the tension among the adults.

"Bitch!" the young man almost yelled at Cherise. "I'm talking to you!"

Angus stepped forward, directly in front of the young man.

"I don't believe she wishes your company at this moment," he informed the lad. "Perhaps you might try at another time."

The lad looked quite angry, but his companions laughed.

"Asshole!" the man shouted at Angus. "Get out of my face or I'll cut you in half!"

Angus smiled. "Others have tried," he informed the lad, "and maybe you will succeed. You'll never know until you try."

The lad's face showed confusion. His companions began to shuffle about, unsure of where this confrontation was leading.

Angus waited.

After a long pause, the young man turned and headed towards his troop. "I ain't got time for you." After moving a safe distance away, he called back, "Next time you won't be so lucky."

Angus smiled.

"Spirited young men," he observed to Charise, who was staring at him.

She shook her head as if to clear away her thoughts, and then looked quite serious. "They could have hurt you," she asserted.

"Maybe," he said, unconcerned. "But there were only five, so I doubt it."

"Really," she said, sounding slightly put out. "You should be careful."

"Ma'am," he said, trying to console her. "I have faced things far more dangerous than a few high spirited lads," he assured her, "and I'm still here. But more than that," he added, "what kind of man would let the likes of them bother a woman and child?"

"Thank you," she said finally. "I don't mean to be ungrateful, but I was concerned about you."

"Thank you," he replied, "but you needn't fear. Neither I nor Erin..." Angus paused to look at the dog, once again bouncing at the feet of the lass. "Would let things end poorly where you are concerned."

Charise clearly did not understand Angus' faith in the puppy, but she smiled.

Angus saw her concern, but understood that she did not see the 20 foot dragon that hid behind a thin magical screen. He smiled, musing that the lads would have been dragon food had he not been there to intervene. Erin clearly loved the lass, and he knew no one would ever be able to harm her as long as Erin lived in this world.

"It's a shame they don't have mothers like you," he observed, finally. "Young Andrew has the manners of a squire."

It was Charise's turn to be confused, but she knew Angus was paying both her and her son a very high compliment.

"He's a good boy," she said quietly.

"He's a fine lad, well-schooled in manners," he observed honestly. "And he learns his lessons well. He has great potential. That's why we come here in the afternoons. Here we build the man who can use those lessons and manners to full advantage."

Angus sensed Charise's concern.

"In my homeland," he explained, "many young lads were sent by their mothers and fathers to learn from me. Many excellent lads became fine young men under my tutelage, but none finer than your Andrew. He has a strong spirit and active mind. He will be great someday."

Charise could sense Angus' sincerity.

"I hope so," she said.

"You should never doubt it," he assured her. "It has been my honor to know him, and I would be proud to continue his lessons in manhood." Pausing, he added, "But only with your approval."

Charise found herself unexplainably drawn to the old man. Perhaps it was his chivalrous intervention with the neighborhood gang, or perhaps it was his flattery of her son. Even yet, she felt she had to make herself clear.

"If you want to help him work out, run, and all that.... fine," she said. "And I believe you are an honest man. But he is my son, and I will teach him what he needs to know about life, so just be a coach and don't try to be a Dad."

Charise was surprised that she had been so direct. She wanted to say that she would kill anyone who hurt her son, but she somehow couldn't bring herself to say such a thing to the old man. And, for reasons she did not understand, she knew Andrew would be safe with him.

But she had lived too long in a hateful world to trust anyone, no matter what her instincts told her. She prayed she was right about this man; for her own sake, as well as Andrew's.

When Andrew came home that evening, she told him it was fine to hang out with Angus. Just keep your wits about you, she told him, and you know the difference between right and wrong.

Andrew was confused but happy. He assured his mother he knew what she was talking about, and that she needn't worry.

That evening Andrew ran with Angus. They followed the sidewalk downtown, then down the side streets to the park. Without stopping, they ran the jogging path, then home. Andrew did not realize he had run seven miles in just over an hour. In fact, he realized very little as he fell on his bed and dropped instantly into a deep sleep.

He was so tired he would not remember his dreams of the land of dragons.

But Erin remembered them well, for his dreams were her dreams.

He was becoming a dragonslayer.

◆◆◆

The Legend of Seth

Chapter the Fifth

When Angus had arrived in this strange world, Andrew had measured his time as 15 years. Andrew had brought Angus strange bread, known as "cake", and it had been delicious. On his 16th birthday, Andrew had invited Angus to his party, and there was not only cake but ice cream and sweet ale called "cola".

Angus would never feel at home in this world, but he had to concede that such things as cake, ice cream, and cola were truly wonderful.

Angus knew little of time in the sense that it was known in this world. In his world, there was no measure of time beyond the time of day or the various seasons. No one counted their summers; that would be like counting the leaves that fall from the trees each autumn. Boys became men when their time had come, but there was no importance attached to their progress; it happened when it happened. Here, much importance was attached not only to seasons and the progress of the sun, but even to smaller increments such as hours and minutes. Angus understood the measures, but could not comprehend the importance attached to them.

Andrew was becoming a man, though, whether measured by the hair on his face or by the passing of years. He was tall, straight and strong. He was doing well in his lessons, whether from his mother, his school, or Angus. There was no doubt that he would become a fine man, and Angus occasionally wished he could take Andrew back to the land of dragons, where he would no doubt become a fine dragonslayer.

Several times a week, he watched Andrew play the game Dragon's Tale. Andrew was now facing bright green dragons, and he was consistently victorious. Even though in this world the battle was not mortal combat, he could see the fine improvement in Andrew's strategies and marveled at his increasing stamina. Andrew seemed to respond at the end in almost the way a dragonslayer would respond in Angus' world. Euphoria followed by fatigue was so familiar to Angus, he never wondered why a game would induce the same effect.

Erin's scales had turned blue, and her magic puppy persona had grown to a full size dog. Angus was comforted that she continued to be good hearted and obviously adored Andrew, his mother Charise, and the girl Latisha.

Angus, Erin and Andrew were on their afternoon run when they entered the park and Andrew stopped unexpectedly. Angus followed his gaze and saw some young boys playing the game he had learned was "basketball". Several young men had entered the court, and a confrontation seemed to be taking shape.

Andrew ran toward the boys. Angus and Erin followed.

As Andrew ran onto the court, Angus stopped at the gate and motioned for Erin to remain at his side. He sensed this was to be a conflict, but he wanted to see how Andrew comported himself.

Andrew moved quickly between the leader of the young men and the boys who had been playing.

"Leave them alone," he said to the leader.

"You need to stay out of this," the leader said, menacingly.

Erin started to move, but Angus stopped her.

"You need to leave them alone," Andrew replied simply, "they're just kids. They got nothing you want."

"Maybe not," said the leader, reaching into the front of his trousers, "but that's for me to decide. You need to get your punk ass out of my way and leave us alone, or I'll send you home in a bag."

Andrew moved suddenly toward the man, knocking him to the ground. Angus saw a dull black object in Andrew's hand, and knew without question he had disarmed the other man in a single move.

The others backed away as Andrew looked from face to face.

"You're going to need another one of these if you're going to take me on," Andrew said quietly, holding the black object in front of him and pointing to the man on the ground. "Do we finish this here, or do you want to wait for another day?"

The man on the ground crab-walked away from Andrew. When he had moved several yards away, he rolled and jumped to his feet.

"You have no idea who you're messing with!" he shouted at Andrew.

Angus heard a metallic click across the courtyard.

"Then let's finish this," Andrew said quietly.

The man and his band began backing away from Andrew. After several yards, they turned and stormed toward the gate where Angus and Erin waited. Angus stepped back to let them pass, but Erin faced them and growled.

Angus looked at Erin and willed her away from their path. This match was over, and Andrew was clearly the victor. He did not want

Erin to reopen the argument, even if the outcome would surely be in her favor.

The boys passed, keeping a careful eye on Erin and hardly noticing Angus.

Andrew looked at the young boys and told them to go back to their game. Then he walked over to Angus and Erin. He was holding the black object close to his belt as if to hide it.

When he reached the gate, Angus asked, "Is that what they call a gun?"

Andrew nodded solemnly. Then he saw two constables come around the corner of a nearby building, and began looking around for a place to dispose of the weapon.

"Give it to Erin," Angus said softly.

Andrew held the gun down and Erin took it in her mouth. Throwing her head back, she swallowed it in one gulp.

The constables approached and told Andrew to put his hands on the fence. He did so, and one officer began patting him all over his body. When he reached Andrew's ankles, he stood back next to the other constable. Neither constable seemed to notice Angus; their attention was on Andrew.

"We got a call," one said, "that someone was harassing the kids here. Was that you?" the first constable asked.

"No, sir," Andrew replied respectfully. "There were some guys here, but they left."

"And you're not one of them?" the constable inquired.

"No, sir," Andrew replied. "We were just out for a run and came over to watch the game while we caught our breath."

Finally, the second constable looked at Angus.

"Is that so?" he asked.

"Yes," Angus replied.

The two constables conferred quietly. Then the first one approached the boys playing basketball. Apparently satisfied with their answer, he returned.

"Let's see some ID," he said to both Angus and Andrew.

Andrew withdrew his leather purse and provided a shiny piece of paper to the constable. The second constable watched Angus, who did not move.

"He's with me," Andrew said to the constable. "He's from England or somewhere. He probably doesn't bring an ID when we are out running."

Angus followed Andrew's lead.

"I'm sorry, sir," he said, "but I do not bring papers with me when I run. Should I?" "Yes, you should," replied the constable, clearly perturbed by the turn of events. "But I'll let it go this time."

Angus thanked the constable, which seemed to make him happy.

"You guys need to be careful when you run," he said. "We've been having some gang activity around here, and it's getting rougher all the time." Pausing, he added, "We can't be everywhere, so try to stay away from anything that looks like a gang when you're out. And don't be running after dark."

Both Angus and Andrew thanked him for his advice.

As the constables departed, Angus, Andrew and Erin returned to their run. They passed around the glade on the jogging track, and then ran back to their building. Andrew parted company as he reached his own door, while Angus and Erin went to their quarters.

In the quiet of his quarters, Angus sat in a chair and pondered the events of the afternoon. Erin, sensing that Angus was deeply troubled, sat next to him on the floor.

After a while, Angus closed his eyes and sought to visualize Garand. He had no idea if he could contact the old sorcerer, but he had to try. In just a moment, he could see Garand standing before him, holding a tall staff.

"Thank you for coming," Angus thought, reaching for the vision.

"You are troubled," Garand responded.

"Aye," affirmed Angus.

Neither spoke for a few moments, as Garand's image became clearer to Angus. When it was as if he were standing before Angus, Garand looked at Erin.

"Her scales are turning blue," he observed.

"Aye," Aaron answered. "And the lad has become a dragonslayer."

Garand looked surprised. Angus remained silent as Garand's gazed passed back and forth, first looking at the old dragonslayer, then the dragon. Finally, the old sorcerer looked at Angus and asked, "How do you know?"

"He has the moves," Angus replied. "Not the moves of a novice, but the moves of a dragonslayer. He knows fear, but he uses it to sharpen his wits. He knows danger from afar, and seeks it out. He answers the call of honor, without hesitation."

Garand sighed, and then looked off into the distance.

"There is a legend," he said, "of the sorcerer Seth. His magic was great, but he grew tired of the endless slaying of dragons, and of men. The legend tells that he left our world when his favorite dragon was slain, and has not been seen again."

"Could young Andrew be his legacy?" asked Angus.

"I do not know," Garand observed. "It would seem possible, for in this world even Seth would have become subject to the passage of time."

Angus nodded knowingly, moving his fingers and feeling the strange stiffness that had developed in his joints. In his own world, he had known little of the pain, associated with aging, which was so pervasive in this world.

Garand tilted his head slightly, as if listening for a far-away voice. Angus waited patiently.

"I do not know if young Andrew might be his legacy," Garand finally stated, "nor do the other sorcerers have any insight into the matter. In our world, neither dragonslayer nor sorcerer may father offspring, but we know not what this world might change of our order.

"Seth was of the southern lands, beyond the deserts, where jungles reach to the sky and mighty rivers roar across the continent. His magic was strong, but he kept to himself and tended his villages alone. We do not know the depth of his magic, nor do we know if he might have passed his magic to an heir, or even found a way to pass it without having offspring."

Garand shook his head solemnly.

"We just do not know. Nor can we advise on how the young dragonslayer will fare in that world. But we do note," he said as if becoming fatigued, "that the yellow scale has turned blue. Clearly," he mused, "some magic is at work there."

Angus waited. The image of the sorcerer faded, and then returned with full clarity. Finally, Angus asked, "What shall I do?"

"Continue as you have," the sorcerer said, finally. "I will go to the southern lands and seek what legends may be there of Seth. I will return when I have something to report, or if there are no legends to be heard."

As the image faded, Angus felt tired. He had never worried, for in his world the dragonslayer's lot was cast with the first dragon. There was no need to worry, for if a dragonslayer were to worry, it would only distract him, and hurry the inevitable day he would not be good enough and the fire would take him.

But worry he did. For young Andrew had come to know the power of being a dragonslayer without ever facing mortal combat. Unlike the young men who learned under Angus' tutelage in the other world, he had never faced the choice of being a dragonslayer, or seeking a less challenging occupation. He did not know what it was to be a dragonslayer, beyond the boundaries of the game which Angus now suspected to be its own form of magic.

Andrew knew not. And Angus could not help him, for Angus knew little more than Andrew.

◆◆◆◆

Latisha

Chapter the Sixth

Angus had no idea what a "full ride" might be, but young Andrew was quite excited about receiving one at the local academy known as the "junior college". It apparently marked very high achievement by Andrew, which did not surprise Angus at all.

There was to be a celebration of sorts at Andrew's academy, and Charise had made a personal trip to Angus' quarters to invite him to attend. Latisha was being unruly, which surprised Angus; the child seemed almost cherubic when he saw her. She would visit with Mrs. Washington, a fine elderly lady in their building, until the adults returned from the celebration.

It was a rare event for Angus to go anywhere without Erin, but she sat quietly by the door when he left. Angus could feel the dragon's emotions if they were strong, and he sensed no anxiety from Erin, so he went to gather Charise and Andrew for the festival.

Andrew, Charise and Angus walked Latisha to Mrs. Washington's apartment. Angus could tell Mrs. Washington enjoyed the girl's company, and Latisha seemed happy to be with her. Charise asked her, again, if she would go, and she said no; it was Andrew's night, and he should enjoy it without her.

The adults headed off for the festivities.

As the pretty lady turned the letters on the game show, Mrs. Washington sat in her recliner with Latisha in a chair next to her. She was happy to have any company, and the young girl's presence made her especially happy. She and the late Mr. Washington had five children, but they were all so busy these days that they rarely visited. Even her grandchildren had gotten older, and they were not as much fun as they had been when they were tykes. Mrs. Washington was always happy when Latisha would come to see her, and it was a rare treat to spend time with her while her mother was away.

As one show ended and the next began, Latisha laid her hand on Mrs. Washington's arm. It was so comforting and so peaceful, the old lady thought. How wonderful to have a chance to spend time with such a lovely child...

As Mrs. Washington rejoiced about having her small charge, she fell asleep and dreamed of the days when she and Mr. Washington were young and newly married. It was a beautiful dream, and she smiled in the real world as her dreams took her to a happy place.

Latisha stood and walked directly to the door. Without hesitating, she opened the door and headed down the hallway to the stairs.

Erin was waiting when Latisha opened the door and let her out.

Child and dog walked into the twilight together. They seemed to know where they were going, and the child sang little songs as the dog bounded next to her. The peacefulness and sweetness of the two seemed incongruent with the dirty, violent neighborhood they walked through.

From the stolen van in the parking lot, Thomas Ketchum watched intently.

Thomas had to be inconspicuous, because the police were always harassing him. He had been sent up the river for ten years because they caught him having sex with a ten year old boy. In prison, he learned that he would have never been caught if he had known to use stolen vehicles. Thomas preferred little boys, but young girls could be interesting as well. As the child turned the corner around the last building, he started the van and moved out carefully.

Latisha stopped, picking up a stick. Carelessly, she threw it and Erin ran retrieve it. They lingered several minutes, forcing Thomas to pass them and circle the block. He needed them to move away from the apartments; you never knew when some do-gooder would intervene at the wrong moment. He stopped short of where the girl and dog played, becoming more excited every time her skirt would swirl as she tossed the stick.

Eventually, they tired of the game and continued down the sidewalk. At the end of the apartment complex was a building which was being renovated. There were many dark hallways and no one to interfere, and Thomas prayed she would walk that far.

Amazingly, Latisha walked right in front of the building and stopped, bending over to scratch her dog behind its ears. Thomas was ecstatic as he parked his van two buildings back and circled around behind the apartments on foot. If she would just stay there for a few minutes....

Thomas wasn't worried about the dog. Pets were rarely a threat to him, since they were usually so timid they ran away if he only yelled at them. Guard dogs were different; but you couldn't pet a dog constantly and expect it to become fierce when there was real danger.

No, the dog was no problem. Thomas just needed to get that young girl a little closer to the building, and then they could play.

When Thomas cut through the stairwell of the construction site, his heart fell. Latisha and her dog were no longer in front of the building. He had been sure they would stay long enough for him to catch them, but they were not there.

Carefully, he slipped through the shadows to get a better look. Looking back and forth, he saw nothing. Somehow, they had gotten away while he was behind the buildings.

The pent up excitement turned to anger. Thomas was furious that the little bitch had gotten away when he least expected it.

Slipping back through the shadows, he re-entered the stairwell. Perhaps, he thought, if he hurried along the back of the building, he could catch her at the next parking lot. It was a fifty-fifty chance; she might have headed back the way she came, but he doubted it. That way was lit fairly well, and he hadn't seen her walking. So she had gone on into the darkness, and maybe he could catch her before she got to the little strip mall that lay just beyond this building and its very dark parking lot.

As he turned and prepared to hurry through the stairwell, he saw the girl. She was standing in the middle of the sidewalk at the back of the building.

Thomas caught his breath. This was truly unexpected, but a very fortunate turn of events. His heart raced as he decided how to handle this opportunity.

"Hi," she said, totally unconcerned about being confronted in the dark by an unknown man. Something in Thomas' mind said to be careful, but the excitement of the moment overcame that instinct.

"Hi," he said, trying to keep his voice calm. "Are you lost?"

"Not really," she said. "I wanted to come here and look around during the day, but my mom won't let me. So I thought I'd come here at night instead."

Thomas was so excited he could barely breathe. Slowly, he moved toward her, watching for any sign she had realized her danger. Latisha stood there smiling, swishing the skirt of her dress as she welcomed him like an old friend.

"Can I show you around?" he asked. "I come here nearly every day," he lied, "and I know everything there is to know about this building."

"I don't think so," she said sweetly. "It's not really a good idea to talk to strangers."

Thomas was nearly within striking distance now, but the girl just swished her skirts and stood there. His heart pounded as he began to imaging what he could do once he had her gagged—it would be SO good, feeling her fighting as he ripped away that dress...

Latisha stopped swishing her skirt and looked at him curiously. Thomas stopped where he was, ready to move quickly if she tried to escape. He had done this many times before, and he knew he was too close for her to escape him now.

"You're not afraid, are you?" he teased. Experience had taught him that teasing children often made them ignore their fear.

"Not really," Latisha replied absently.

Thomas moved ahead slowly, looking both ways as he exited the back of the stairwell. There was nothing, and no one, in either direction. Latisha made no move to escape. His heart raced; the muscles in his arms and legs pulled tight as he prepared to make the final move that would bring her under his control.

"Why aren't you afraid?" he teased. He wanted to scare her now; it was time to let her fear build and increase his excitement as he took her, as many times and in as many ways as he wanted. They would find her here tomorrow, but tonight she was his!

"Because I have a dragon," she answered, smiling happily.

"A dragon can't save you now!" he almost shouted as he sprang toward her.

He was wrong.

Thomas had no way of knowing that an adult dragon has a mouth well over six feet long and a tongue as sticky as fly paper. He also did not know that he would fit well into that mouth with nothing hanging out, not even his shoes. What he learned in the final moments of his life was that a dragon can take a grown man into its mouth and, with a single swallow, push him into acid and heat just like the hell fire and brimstone he had heard about in the churches of his youth. The thought did not last long, for he went into shock well before he died from suffocation in the heat and sulfuric contents of the dragon's stomach.

Within a minute, Thomas was nothing more than a small bubble of gas. When Erin burped a small flame, Latisha giggled and Erin smiled.

Walking back to the sidewalk, they continued their journey past the building and into the strip mall that waited past its very dark parking lot. Thomas' stolen van would soon run out of gas, and the police would impound it in a couple of days.

Thomas' parole officer would be the only one to miss him, and he would wait little more than a month before reporting him as a fugitive and placing him on the very long list of pedophiles who are unaccounted for. He speculated that he would again see Thomas

Ketchum's name, and it would be in association with a missing or murdered child.

Fortunately, he was wrong. Thomas' days as a predator had come to an end.

Latisha and Erin passed the all night convenience store. She waved at the clerk, who was surprised to see a young girl and her dog out alone in this neighborhood, especially at night. He thought about talking to her, or calling the police, but he didn't want the trouble, so he went back to his adult novel that was just getting interesting.

At the end of the strip mall was an old gas station with a service bay. The station had been closed since long before Latisha was born. Inside, the windows were painted. The only light showing from the old building was under the roll-up door, where little strips of light showed curls of smoke as they crept out into the night.

Latisha walked up to the front door of what had been the sales area. She opened the door easily, and let Erin enter before her. The dog waited patiently as Latisha passed her and reached the service door which went into the old service bay. Without hesitation, she opened that door and walked through, Erin at her heels.

Five young Latinos sat in a semi-circle, passing a joint. They called themselves Gladiatores. They were drinking cheap bourbon and smoking a joint, gathering courage for a raid later tonight. They were going to teach that bastard Andrew to stay out of their way.

Andrew had become a problem for the gang. First, he seemed to have no fear of them; that set a very bad example for others in the neighborhood. Not only had he interfered with their somewhat harmless harassment of the kids on the basketball court, he seemed to show up far too often where they sold drugs to the kids from the local schools. Andrew chased off their customers, and had even begun playing basketball with them during the time the Gladiatores had normally sold the bulk of their drugs.

They had always outwitted the police, but Andrew was a real problem.

On the floor next to each boy was an assault rifle or shotgun. In each waistband, a handgun had been lodged. They knew about Andrew's award ceremony, and were planning to ambush him and that old fart that he hung out with as they walked home. Perhaps, the leader had pointed out, they would have time to take advantage of Andrew's mother, since she would undoubtedly be with them.

All the boys looked up when Latisha entered the room, followed by that stupid dog.

As the leader started to say something, Latisha held her right hand out, her arm level with her shoulder. She turned her hand downward, fingers extended and palm flat. All five boys stared in awe as a light began to glow from the bottom of her palm.

The boys remained silent as Latisha rotated her hand until it faced upward. In her palm was a globe of light which appeared to be about six inches in diameter. No one could look away from that light once their eyes had been drawn to it.

Silently, they stared.

Each of the boys saw, in the light, their own life up to this moment, followed by scenes of violence, jail, pain, and despair. Without a word being spoken, they knew the life they saw was their own. In a blink, the scenes changed, and they saw themselves as older men, eating as a family and playing with children.

Each boy knew, without explanation, that the first scene was their life as they were living it; the second was their life as it could be.

Latisha closed her hand and the light disappeared. Silently, she turned and let Erin out the door to the old sales area. Together they left the old store and walked back to their apartment building. Latisha let Erin into the apartment she shared with Angus, and returned to Mrs. Washington's apartment.

Entering the apartment, she sat in the chair next to Mrs. Washington and placed her hand gently on the old lady's arm. After a moment, Mrs. Washington awoke from her dreams. Looking at the clock on the TV, then at Latisha, she said, "Lord, Child. Look at the time. I'd better feed you before your momma gets back and never lets me sit with you again!"

Latisha helped Mrs. Washington prepare a small meal for two. They sat together with their dinners, talking lightly about Latisha's school and the late Mr. Washington. "There is something special about that girl," the old lady thought, "that makes her so loveable you want to hug her until she pops!"

Just after ten, the adults arrived home. Their walk home had been uneventful.

◆◆◆

Dragons and Dragonslayers

Chapter the Seventh

Angus had learned the adage, "Time marches on," during his stay in the new world. While he still did not understand the importance of such a phrase, he did begin to understand why these strange people were so fascinated by time.

Birthdays were but one of the strange rituals in this world. New Year's Eve, which marked the end on one calendar season and the beginning of another, was widely celebrated as if the first day of the new year would somehow be better than the last day of the former one. Yet Angus saw that people planned their lives based on the calendar, and it gave them a sense of urgency which was missing in his world.

Andrew's enrollment in college took him away from home most of the time now. He was always in a hurry—classes started and stopped at a point in time, the library was open certain hours, and basketball practice lasted from 3:30 to 6:00 pm, five days each week.

Angus began to understand why time was so important to these people—they did most things in temporary groups. In his world, you worked with your family or with Elders like Angus, and everyone moved with the same rhythm. Here, everyone had their own rhythm, and only by setting the time of an activity could the necessary people gather.

Andrew planned his life with a calendar and a watch, and Angus watched in wonder as the lad moved from one thing to the next. Angus knew the lad was progressing well, but he never realized how well until Andrew took him to the basketball court at the junior college late one night when no one else was around.

Standing under the elevated ring—"basket"—Andrew threw the ball through the basket at the other end. Taking ball after ball, Andrew moved to different positions around the court and, each time, threw the ball through the basket.

When he finished, Andrew gathered the balls and returned them to their container—also known as a "basket"-- and sat down on the first row of benches known as "bleachers". Sensing that he was troubled, Angus sat next to the young man.

"Did you see what I just did?" Andrew asked, looking straight ahead.

"Aye, Lad," Angus replied.

"It's impossible," Andrew stated with sadness in his voice. "There are professional basketball players who play every day, who are the best in the world, and none of them could do what I just did. Ten for ten, full court, nothing but net. And," he added, "it's just as easy for me to do a hundred of them as it is to do ten. I always hit what I am aiming at."

"It's not impossible, Lad," Angus replied, puzzled. "You just did it."

"I love basketball," Andrew continued as if he hadn't heard Angus. "The team, the crowd, the thrill of winning. But I have to remember not to play at full steam. I'm too fast, my shots are too accurate, I always know what every player on the floor is going to do before they do it. If I played full-out," he said sadly, "everyone would know I'm a freak."

"You're not a freak," Angus responded quietly, "you're a dragonslayer."

Andrew turned to the old man.

"I don't know how," Angus explained slowly, "and I don't know why. But I've been a dragonslayer for as long as I can remember, and I've trained hundreds of lads who became dragonslayers. You are," he concluded, "one of the best I've ever known. That's why you hit where you shoot, why you move like a rabbit, and why you sense every movement around you."

Andrew was still troubled. "Dragonslayers don't live in this world," he reasoned. "They live in the world of dragons."

"As did I," Angus said quietly, "and the dragon who sleeps next to my bed. But now we are here....and so are you."

Andrew looked away silently for several minutes.

"Ever since you came here," he mused, "everything's gotten better. My grades, my body, my balance...everything. It's like having you here brought out something in me that makes me better than I could ever imagine."

"Don't forget, Lad," Angus reasoned, "you had a hand in it. You run with me, stride for stride, or your body would not be as it is. You spend your time studying in the library or at home, or your grades would not be as they are. I may train dragonslayers," he concluded, "but the work is yours. You deserve everything you have, and more, because you are a good lad who puts his heart into everything he does."

Andrew's eyes filled with tears when the old man put his hand on Andrew's shoulder.

"I'll do this for four years," Andrew finally said, choking back his emotions, "then I'm moving on to something else."

"What do four years have to do with anything?" Angus asked, bewildered by Andrew's decision.

"That's how long college lasts. Two years here at the junior college, then two more at the University. But I'll be just good enough to make my team mates look good," he concluded, "because I don't want to be a professional athlete. I want to be something that matters."

"I don't know what that would be," Angus conceded, "but I'm sure you'll know when the time comes."

Even Angus began to count the years left as Andrew completed community college and moved on to the University.

Time was not standing still for Charise or Latisha, either. Latisha had blossomed into a beautiful young woman, charming all around her with a smile and quick wit. Angus thought Charise became more beautiful each day. He dined with her often as the years went on. They enjoyed each other's company, and Charise had more time as her children grew ever more independent. They went together to Andrew's basketball games during the season, and Angus did not know whether he enjoyed the competition or Charise's company more. At first they drew some stares—the stately black woman towering over the older, red-haired man—but eventually everyone else got used to seeing them together.

The University was much farther from their home than the community college had been, but Angus and Charise often chose to walk home rather than take a taxi or a bus. Angus' purse worked as it always had—never running out of the scraps of paper known as "dollars"—but they enjoyed the time and Charise felt oddly safe when accompanied by the older man.

The night of the division finals—which Andrew's team had won by two points—Erin was waiting outside the exit doors when Angus and Charise walked out. It was unusual for her to be there, but there had been other games where she had walked out to greet them, so Charise petted her head and the three walked away together.

As they passed along a poorly-lit section lined by empty stores, Angus felt the hair on his neck begin to rise. Glancing down at Erin, he could see that she was walking with more determination, and her head moved back and forth, looking for whatever might lie ahead. Angus instinctively moved closer to Charise, and she smiled down at him as he did.

A black man stepped out of an empty doorway, blocking their path.

"Hey, Mama," he said tauntingly. "The old guy paying your bills?" Pausing, he added with a sinister tone, "Maybe he needs to pay a few of mine."

From behind him, two others stepped out.

"Yeah," one said, "and maybe you can pay me with some of what you been payin' him!"

Angus smiled and stepped forward, placing himself between Charise and the men. He motioned for Erin to stand with Charise, and she slid over quietly.

Just as he was about to speak, Angus saw eleven more shadows move behind the first three. The smile left his face.

The first man stepped forward, intending to push Angus. Instead, Angus grabbed his arm and pulled him off balance to Angus' right side. As he passed, Angus held on to the arm as it twisted out of its socket. The pain was clear in the man's cry.

Bedlam erupted when the leader hit the ground. In the back of the group, one man pulled a gun and swung it toward Angus. Before he could bring the weapon to bear, he was speared through the heart and left lung by a twenty inch long knife. As the man fell forward on the four inch handle, he wondered where the knife had come from—he never saw the knife, and he definitely didn't see the man throw it.

Charise stood mesmerized as Angus went through the crowd of men. He moved as if he had choreographed the fight—standing close to one while kicking another in the head; then turning on the one closest to him and twisting his head sharply enough to snap his neck. One by one, he plowed through the crowd. Charise knew that most of the wounds were lethal—she had seen enough trauma in her life to know the difference.

Angus pushed one man aside as he kicked the feet from under another. As the man's head crushed against the sidewalk, the first man sprinted away from Angus—right into Charise. Instead of moving or being run over, she grabbed him and stepped back with her left foot as her right knee slammed into his groin. The man hit the ground hard, knocking him unconscious as he held tightly to his groin.

When it was over, Angus rolled the gunman over to retrieve his long knife. He wiped the blade on the front of the young man's shirt, leaving an X of blood streaks. The body count was 12 dead, 2 wounded. The leader lay on the ground, conscious but with a dislocated shoulder. The other survivor lay unconscious, still holding his groin.

Angus pushed his knife back in its scabbard, shielded again by the magic screen between his self and the image available to those of this world. As he approached Charise, she drew back.

"What...happened?" she asked, appalled at the carnage.

"We call them highwaymen," Angus replied.

Angus looked to Erin, who quietly walked over and licked the face of the man with the dislocated shoulder. Almost immediately, he looked confusedly at Angus and Charise.

"What happened?" he asked, as if he had not heard Charise's question or Angus' answer.

Erin was on her way to the groin-injured man, who regained consciousness as she licked him in the face. Like the first man, he looked confused as he scanned the bodies around him.

"Must have been a gang fight," Angus replied to the injured man. "You want us to call you an ambulance?"

"No," the man said quickly, trying to rise using his remaining arm. "We'll be OK."

"I don't think so," Angus commented. As he took Charise's elbow, he added, "but we'll be moving along before there is any more violence."

"Yeah," the man answered, still dazed. "You do that."

Charise's sense of self-preservation made her move with Angus and Erin as they walked quietly away from the scene. But every step she took made her blood boil more, and as they reached a safe distance and were crossing a public park, she exploded.

"What the HELL happened back there?"

"They were going to rob us, kill me, and probably rape you," Angus said matter-of-factly. "I couldn't let them do that. If I had simply wounded them, they would have hunted us down later, and I might not have been there to protect you. So they had to die."

"I got all that," Charise said angrily. "What's with the dog licking those guys and all of a sudden they have a lobotomy?"

"Can I tell you when we are home?" Angus asked as sirens loomed closer.

"No."

"Well," Angus stalled.

"Come on," Charise demanded.

"Well, it's hard to explain," he began, "and harder to believe. But Erin is really a dragon, and her spittle is magic. She made them forget, and they will be confused for some time. It was either dragon spit," he concluded, "or kill them. And I'd had enough of killing."

"Erin is a dragon..." It wasn't really a question; Charise said it like she was trying on the idea. "Well, that would explain a lot."

Angus looked at her carefully, trying to figure out what she was thinking. Even with his magically enhanced senses, he was at a loss.

"What does she normally look like?" Charise asked.

Angus was at a loss. How does one describe a dragon? Finally, he looked around them; no one was in sight. He looked down at Erin. Within a second, the beagle disappeared and a twenty foot, green scale dragon stood by his side.

Charise blinked her eyes slowly, then smiled.

Erin returned to her beagle persona.

Looking at Angus, she asked, "Do you look like you, or are you a mirage as well?"

Angus looked at Erin again, and she removed the magical screen. After about 30 seconds, it returned.

"OK," Charise said. "Let's go home."

Silence ruled the journey home. When they arrived at the apartment building, Angus walked Charise to her door. As he turned to leave, she urged him, "No. Come in. Please?"

Walking into the apartment, Charise called, "Latisha! Andrew!"

No one answered.

Charise turned to Angus and said, "Wait here."

When she returned, Charise was carrying an artist's sketch pad. She stopped two feet in front of Angus and Erin, and held the pad in front of her. When she lifted the front cover, Angus was amazed— it was a perfect drawing of Garth! Erin barked and jumped up and down—apparently, she recognized her father as well.

Charise turned page after page, and each page contained another drawing or painting of Garth. The quality of the first drawing was excellent, but they continued to improve as she flipped through the pages.

On the last page was a picture of Garth with a young yellow-scale next to him. Angus recognized the yellow scale as Erin.

Angus was speechless.

After a long and awkward silence, Charise said, "I drew them when I was a girl in school. I drew other things, but I saved this pad exclusively for dragons. Always the same dragon, until the last picture, when I drew in a baby."

"The baby is Erin," Angus told her, "and the dragon is Garth, her father!"

Charise put the pad at the end of the couch, then sat next to it. She motioned for Angus to sit in the rocker he normally occupied after dinner, when they would talk. Erin lay down next to the pad, looking happily at the final drawing.

After a long silence, Charise shook her head as if to clear her thoughts. "I don't know how I could have drawn Erin and her father. Do you?"

Angus shook his head. "No," he said, "but I know someone who might. I will contact him and hope he has an answer."

Charise nodded. After a short pause, she asked, "Those men back there. You said you were tired of killing. How many men have you killed?"

Angus looked pained. "Twelve," he replied. "All of them tonight."

Charise looked surprised, so Angus added, "In my world, no one would dare attack a dragonslayer. We are trained to fight dragons, so men are minor challenges. Plus we have magic." Thinking for a moment, he added with a note of sadness, "I am the most elder of the dragonslayers, so I have the most skill and the most magic of them all. Until tonight, though, I have never had to use my skills on men."

They sat quietly for an hour, lost in their thoughts while Erin gazed happily on the drawing. When Latisha came home, Charise put away the artist's pad and they chatted lightly for a few minutes before Angus and Erin took their leave.

When he returned to his room, Angus sat in his chair with Erin on the floor beside him. Closing his eyes, he called out for Garand. When the sorcerer appeared, Angus opened his memories to let the Sorcerer see the evening as he had. When he was done, the Sorcerer thought silently for several minutes.

"We must speak face-to-face," he said finally. "There is much magic, and I will need to see you to understand it all and, hopefully, we can understand it together."

Angus nodded.

"Go to the mountains in the East," Garand continued. "Take Erin with you. I will find you there, and we can take counsel in private."

"Aye," Angus replied. "I will leave at first light."

◆◆◆◆

Moments of Truth

Chapter the Eighth

The morning sun was just a glow in the eastern sky, shining through the smog, when Angus and Erin left the apartment complex. They walked toward the glow, moving through the buildings while only a few people were awake and about.

As they left the clusters of large buildings and walked toward the hills, Angus saw the houses disappear as Erin became a dragon. They had returned to the land of dragons, and open glades and forested hills replaced the streets and houses of the other world.

Within the hour, they had arrived at an open meadow where Garand sat on a fallen tree, awaiting their arrival.

"Good morning," Garand greeted them. "You look well." He nodded to both Angus and Erin.

Angus returned the nod but said nothing. He was waiting for the old sorcerer to open the conversation.

Garand looked first to Erin.

"I see you've grown your green scales," he complimented her. "Congratulations."

Erin briefly nodded her head in acknowledgement.

Turning to Angus, Garand opened the conversation. "Much has happened, old friend, and we must discuss it to see if we can determine what it all means."

Angus sat on the log next to Garand. Erin looked about impatiently. Garand noted the green scale's impatience, and offered, "If you wish, you can hunt yourself some breakfast while we talk."

Erin looked at Angus, who nodded. Quickly, she took flight and was out of sight within moments.

The two men looked at each other, each wondering where to begin.

Meanwhile, in the other world, the school day had begun. Within the first hour, Latisha walked into the office and told the school secretary, "I need to leave."

The secretary began to ask for a note, and then reconsidered. Taking the sign out log, she made the appropriate entries. Without further discussion, Latisha left the office. The secretary wondered, momentarily, why she had not asked for a permission slip, and then decided it wasn't worth worrying about. Placing the sign-out book back into its basket, she returned to her daily activities.

Carlos Laguna had been cruising about all morning in his taxi, but fares were few and far between on the sunny morning. It was to be expected; when the weather was good, most of his fares would walk, or wait at a bus stop, rather than pay the extra money to take a taxi. With no sign of rain, he expected a slow morning.

As he passed the high school, Carlos decided to cruise the front of the building in case anyone there needed a cab. It was a long shot, but there was nothing else going on, so he turned into the circular drive.

Amazingly, a teenage girl was standing under the awning in front of the building, flagging him down.

Stepping into the taxi as if she had done it hundreds of times, she gave Carlos an address. Normally he would ask about the fare money, but this time he just nodded and drove away.

Arriving in front of the apartment complex at the address the girl had given him, Carlos stopped. The fare was $13.50, but the girl handed him a twenty and told him to keep the change.

"I have a friend who needs a cab," she said, opening the door and swinging her legs out. "If you wait just a minute, I think you can make a good fare off her, too."

"Thanks," Carlos answered, tucking the twenty into his shirt pocket. "I'll wait here for a few, in case she's still here."

"Oh, she's still here...." Latisha smiled and waved before walking away from the taxi and into the building.

Within minutes, a gorgeous 40-something woman exited the door where the girl had entered the building. She was wearing clothes much too nice for this neighborhood, and Carlos instinctively knew she would want to go much farther than the little girl's school. Maybe she's a good tipper, too, Carlos thought optimistically.

As the woman entered his cab, Carlos couldn't help but stare. She was strikingly beautiful, a mocha-skinned beauty wearing a designer dress and shoes, an outfit that probably cost as much as Carlos' cab. He was surprised she was using a taxi instead of a limo, but that was just another bit of good luck for him.

Instead of an address, the lady instructed him to get on an eastbound highway. As a rule, Carlos wanted a final address, but as he turned to explain, the lady smiled and his heart melted. Without further instructions, Carlos turned to drive away.

"Don't forget the meter," the lady said sweetly.

Carlos dropped the flag on his meter. Funny, he thought; I've never forgotten that before.

After heading east, Carlos' fare gave instructions on exits and turns taking them into the hills. The meter passed $100 as she instructed him to turn up a dirt road that wandered into the undeveloped foothills. Ten minutes later, she told him, "Stop here."

Carlos looked around. There was nothing to be seen but rocks and scrub bushes all around. Turning to ask her if she was sure she wanted to stop here, he was again silenced by her smile.

"Here," she said sweetly, handing him three bills. "I need to you wait, if you can. This should cover the trip and your time."

Carlos looked at the three $100 bills in his hand and nodded.

The woman left the cab and walked up the hill, picking her way among the rocks and scrub like an experienced mountain climber. Apparently, her three thousand dollar Italian heels didn't bother her, even in this terrain.

Without even wondering why he was here or what the woman was up to, Carlos laid his seat back for a nap while the meter cheerfully clicked of the charges for his waiting time.

As she passed from the view of the cab, the woman's designer clothes transformed to a harambe with an elaborate matching shawl and traditional walking sandals. Within minutes, she walked into the meadow where Angus and Garand were sitting.

Both men stood as she approached. As if on cue, Erin landed next to the fallen tree, facing the newcomer.

"Greetings," she said as she reached the men. "I am Ayana, envoy of Seth."

Ayana bowed her head slightly, then looked at Angus. "Greetings, Angus, Slayer of Garth, Elder of all Dragonslayers."

Angus silently returned the bow.

"Greetings, Garand the Fair, Sorcerer of the Central Provinces."

The sorcerer stared but did not return the bow. Angus looked at the sorcerer's face and could tell he was concentrating on the newcomer. Angus could clearly tell that the sorcerer was not pleased with the visitor.

The smile left Ayana's face. Sighing, she looked at Garand and said, "Don't trifle with me, old man. I am an emissary from Seth, and while I may not have Seth's full powers, I am more than a match for your magic. Otherwise, how could I have found this glade and entered without your knowledge?"

Garand looked thoughtful for a moment, and then nodded in respect.

Without waiting for a verbal response, Ayana added, "I have been sent to make certain events clear to you, and to offer Seth's counsel on the future course of events."

Ayana waited for Garand to respond.

"Welcome," he said finally. "Any enlightenment is welcome, and we value the counsel of the great Seth."

Ayana held her hand out to Erin, who lay her monstrous head in Ayana's hand. Angus could feel the happiness glow from the dragon as Ayana stroked her with her left hand and scratched Erin's chin with the right.

"My precious Erin," Ayana cooed to the dragon, "you have grown to such a beautiful dragon. Your father would be most proud."

There was something familiar about this woman, and the joyous way Erin reacted, but Angus could not quite place it. When Ayana gave a final pat to Erin's head, the dragon reluctantly stood again to her full height.

"Let us sit and take counsel," Ayana offered. As if on cue, Erin grasped a large boulder in her mouth and placed it behind the woman. Ayana nodded and smiled, and the dragon smiled back. After Ayana was comfortably seated, the men returned to their placed on the log.

"Some of what seems strange to you," Ayana began without prompting, "is just the natural result of having a concentration of magic outside its natural boundaries. Angus has a great deal of magic within and around him, as we all know. The magic of ten thousand dragons and, especially, the magic of the great Garth. He lives in a magic bubble which hides his identity from those around him. That magic, in a world where magic rarely resides, is bound to change the world around him."

The men nodded, acknowledging that neither of them had seriously considered this before.

"And," Ayana continued, "Erin is a very special dragon, the offspring of Garth, greatest of all dragons. It is she that created and maintains the illusionary bubble around herself and Angus. This magic, too, has its effects on those around her.

"All of this you would have understood, given time to ponder it, because you know of the magic and can see how its affects cannot be completely limited to those it is intended to protect."

Ayana paused, waiting until the men indicated understanding before she continued.

"What you could not know," she added, "because Seth has hidden it from you, is that Charise is not an ordinary woman. Her birth name is Amira, and she is a descendant of King Solomon and Sheba through their son, Ebna la-Hakim. She has little magic of her own, but she is quite responsive to the magic around her.

"When she was but a child, her homeland became very dangerous for those of royal descent. Her mother, who knew of the World of Dragons, arranged to move here with the child and remained several seasons until she decided what to do. Mother and child returned to their own world at a location far from their homeland, and that's where Amira became Charise. Dangers remain in their homeland, and there are dangers in this world for her, so Charise must be protected."

Looking at Angus, she added, "The Elder has done an admirable job, even though he did not know that it was his fate to do so."

Angus smiled and responded, "It was my pleasure."

Ayana smiled back. "The boy, Andrew, is also a descendant of Solomon and Sheba. Interestingly, his father was a descendant of Seth. The magic you see in the boy has always been there, but Angus has brought it out and given it direction."

"It was no accident," she said to Angus, "that you were exiled to the world of Andrew, or that you met him when you did. Garth knew, when he went to the field of battle, that he would ultimately face you, and that you would prevail. Seth loved Garth above all other dragons, and Garth was honored to lay down his life in Seth's service. Seth regrets that you have been placed at peril without your knowledge or consent, but prior disclosure was not an acceptable option."

Angus nodded his head in understanding.

"That is the truth, so far," Ayana concluded. Looking to Garand, she said, "Perhaps it is time we tell the Elder the truth about the dragon wars and the dangers that have emerged in his world."

Angus looked at Garand. Garand sighed, looking at Ayana. Ayana's face showed determination, so Garand turned to Angus.

"Legend tells that the dragons attacked villages and towns," Garand began, "and the dragon slayers formed and trained to protect humans from the dragons. Eventually, the dragons and dragonslayers began to face each other on the field of battle, rather than in response to an attack by the dragons."

"Aye," Angus affirmed.

"In days of old, dragons did attack the villages," Garand affirmed, "but they were not dragons such as Erin, here. They were dragons from beyond the eastern provinces. Dragons without magic. They had been trained as a tool of war by the warlords of those lands. The warlords had conquered all the lands beyond our eastern provinces by using the dragons as an initial attack, terrifying and scattering the villagers.

"As the sorcerers from the provinces watched the carnage to our east, we knew it was simply a matter of time before the warlords attacked us. We had dragons, but they were like Erin; peaceful, playful, and disinterested in war. Try as we might, we could not get our dragons to come to our aid, and we awaited the inevitable slaughter which would come when the warlords turned to the west.

"One day an emissary, much like Ayana, came to us from Seth. We were offered battle dragons, which were bred for, and trained, in warfare. No compensation was requested, and no conditions placed on the loan. Seth simply did not want us to be annihilated like the people beyond our eastern frontier.

'Of course, we accepted, and Seth's dragons arrived just prior to the attack from the East. They defeated the dragons from the east and routed the armies before a single land battle had occurred."

"It was inevitable," Garand continued, "that Seth's dragons mated with our dragons before they returned to the lands beyond the deserts. The result is what you see next to you," he concluded, pointing at Erin. "Great dragons, full of magic, who develop from the yellow scaled babies to the great green scales of a proven warrior."

Garand held his hands out, palms up. "To get the dragons to mature into warriors, we had to provide them with battles. To develop an army of trained warrior humans, we created the legends and began the practice of having dragons and dragonslayers meet on the field of battle. This gave the dragons courage and aggression, while training men who shared the dragon's magic and were trained for battle. This was the scheme of the sorcerers to maintain security without a standing Army."

Angus stared at Garand. Everything he had ever learned, or believed, had been crushed by the old Sorcerer's story.

"We did the best we could," Garand almost pleaded, seeing the shock on the dragonslayer's face. "We knew that a standing Army would eventually look for something to conquer, just as the warlords had. We needed the dragons to mature. This avoided the potential of the provinces turning on each other and provided a trained, ready group of men and dragons if we were ever again to face an attack." Pausing, he added, "It was the best idea we could come up with at the time."

Angus was not given to anger; anger distracted, and dragonslayers learned early not to be distracted or they would be short-lived. Nonetheless, he felt fury at the lies and betrayals of the sorcerers, and crushing sadness for all the dragons and dragonslayers that had died at the pleasure of a small group of men.

"Tell him the rest," Ayana insisted, looking at Garand.

"The armies of the Far East are again gathering, and we expect them to attack soon," he said, sounding almost defeated. "They have a quarter of a million dragons and about that many soldiers. We have farmers, tradesmen, and a few hundred dragon slayers. And we have no time to bring the dragons into the fight, for they see humans as adversaries."

Silence reigned for several minutes. Angus and Garand were consumed by their own thoughts. Ayana appeared to be waiting.

Finally, Ayana spoke. "Seth is again coming to your aid," she said, "but there is a greater danger than even the armies. The warlords have sent out spies looking for the Orb of Solomon, and they travel both worlds seeking it. If the Orb were to be possessed by the warlords, there is nothing that can be done to save anyone in this world, and the bloodshed may even spill over into the world of science."

Angus and Garand both leaned toward Ayana, as if to hear her better.

"It is said that Solomon was not only wise, but that he could control demons," Ayana began. "That was just a primitive way of saying he controlled magic. According to legend, Solomon prayed for wisdom, but not money or power. He was rewarded with wealth and power beyond his imagination, as well as the wisdom he requested. After a day of administering the largest kingdom in the world of that time, he would lie with dozens of his seven hundred wives and three hundred concubines, fathering hundreds of children.

"His great stamina and potency were credited to a special gift from God. Each night, when he would retire to his own chambers, spent by the demands of the kingdom and his women, he was visited by a magic orb. Having lain with the orb for a few hours, Solomon would emerge more vigorous and potent than any other man in the world.

"When Solomon died, the orb disappeared. In fact, no one had ever seen the orb, but he had mentioned its magic powers to his trusted advisors. Over the centuries, many have searched for the orb, but none have found it.

"Now the warlords are again seeking the orb, as well as gathering their armies and dragons at your borders."

Ayana paused.

"Seth advises that Angus return to this world, bringing Andrew, Charise, and the girl child with him. Andrew must face his fate on the field of battle, and that is an event possible only in this world. As to his mother and the foundling, they will be safer with Angus and Andrew, and Seth loves them both, so he asks Angus for the boon of remaining with them until his fate or theirs separates them."

Angus looked directly into Ayana's eyes. "And if I bring them, how will that stop the war and protect the orb?"

Ayana smiled. "You are a wise and practical man, Angus," she said with fondness. "Seth believes the fate of the orb and the fate of the provinces are intertwined. It seems that Andrew is key to some measure of hope, but how that is true is not yet clear. If you will bring him to the field of battle, then perhaps his ultimate fate will become clear."

"Aye," Angus replied. "I will bring the lad, though his fate weighs heavier on my heart than any other I have trained. I will bring also his mother and the foundling, both of whom I also hold dear." As he stood, Garand and Ayana stood as well.

"Can you carry a message to Seth?" Angus asked Ayana.

"If you wish," she replied.

"Please tell the great Seth," Angus said solemnly, "that the boy's fate will be sealed on the field of battle. But if his mother and Latisha meet their fate in this world or any other, it will mean that both Erin and I have already met ours."

"Understood," Ayana said. Briskly, she turned and walked away from the men.

By the time Ayana reached the cab, she was again in her Italian designer clothes and shoes. Carlos, who had slipped into a peaceful nap, awoke when she opened the door and sat in the back seat. Straightening his seat, he heard her say, "Take me home, please."

The taxi arrived at the apartment complex at lunch time. The meter said $195, but Ayana waived off his offer of change and casually said, "Keep it." Carlos, a happily married man, still enjoyed watching her as she walked to the building and disappeared into the double doors.

As he drove away, Carlos had a deep feeling of good fortune, although his meter said he had taken no fares all morning. He knew he should wonder about the $320 in his shirt pocket, but somehow he couldn't concentrate on it long enough to figure it out. As he turned onto the main boulevard, he decided he'd head home for lunch.

Maybe he'd be lucky, and his kids would all be in school and his wife would be in a good mood. Somehow, this seemed to be his lucky day.

••••

Preparation Begins

Chapter the Ninth

Angus remained in the world of dragons for two days, going over the situation with Garand. There was little to be done about the army forming to the East, but Angus had much to do to prepare Andrew for his trip to the field of battle. Garand returned to the provinces to do what could be done there. Angus returned to the world of science to prepare Andrew and try to convince Charise to accompany him to the world of dragons.

Talking to Andrew had to wait a few days after Angus returned. Andrew was taking a series of "mid-term" exams, and he was very focused on his studies. When exams were done, Angus interrupted their evening run to spend time in the park, bringing Andrew up to date on the information Angus had gained during his trip.

Andrew was concerned about facing a dragon on the field of battle.

"I'm not sure I'm ready to kill a dragon," he confided in Angus.

"We have training to do, but you will be fine," Angus reassured him.

"I'm not afraid I'm not good enough," Andrew explained. "I just don't know I can kill an animal for sport, especially one that looks like Erin."

Angus nodded. "Aye, Lad," he reassured him, "but when you face the fire, I believe you will respond the way you have learned in Dragon's Tale. If we can get you a suitable sword and long knife, you can use my lance."

"Where did you get your sword?" Andrew asked.

"It was made by the dwarves," Angus replied, "but I'm afraid they are busy with their own armaments right now." After thinking for a few moments, he sighed. "We can get you a sword, for many have been left behind by fallen dragon slayers. The problem is that each sword is made for its master, and I don't know how well it will work in your hands. Not only is the weight and length designed for its owner, but each sword has elven script which gives it a bit of magic when the dragon slayer holds the sword."

The two men stood silently for several moments.

"Well, if I can't get one made by a dwarf, I'll get one made by a Fazulo," Andrew announced.

"What, pray tell, is a Fazulo?" Angus asked.

"It's not *what* a Fazulo is," Andrew replied. "It's *who*. **Lorenzo Fazulo.** I go to college with him. He grew up in his father's machine shop, so he knows how to work metal. And he's an exercise physiologist, so I'm pretty sure he can figure out the balance part. As for the magic...." Andrew pondered momentarily. "Well, I'll just have to hope the magic you and Erin bring will be enough."

Angus did not understand what Andrew was talking about, but he had learned to trust the lad when it came to things in his world. Nodding, Angus turned and began his run through the park and beyond to the apartment building, Andrew matching him stride-for-stride.

The next morning, Andrew, Angus, and Erin took a bus to the industrial section of town. Andrew led the way to a large machine shop, which was as noisy and hot as the workshops of the dwarves. Angus was amazed at the number and variety of people working as they walked to the back of the building and into a small office area.

"Hey, Fazulo!" Andrew shouted at a stout young man.

"Yo! Wyatt Earp! What are you doing on the working side of town?" came the reply.

Angus was totally confused by the way the young men greeted each other, but he smiled and shook the young Fazulo's hand. The grip was that of a working man, but the young man's face showed the same bright intelligence Angus has long admired in Andrew.

"I need a favor," Andrew replied after Fazulo let go of Angus' hand. "And it's a whopper. Can you walk?"

Fazulo smiled. "A friend in need is a friend indeed," he replied. "Let's take a stroll".

The three men walked out the back of the shop and along an alley, Erin prancing along behind.

"Remember Dragon's Tale?" Andrew asked Fazulo as they walked.

"Yeah," Fazulo replied, "and I'm still going to kick your ass one of these days."

"You won't want to try that any time soon," Andrew laughed. Turning to Angus, he said, "Show him how you really look."

Angus was concerned about showing his true identity, but he trusted that Andrew had a reason. Turning to Erin, he nodded, and in a blink of an eye he was again Angus the Elder.

Fazulo's expression turned to amazement. "Holy Shit!" he blurted out. "You're the dragonslayer!"

Angus smiled and bowed. A moment later, his image changed back to the one he used in Andrew's world.

"Which brings me to the favor," Andrew ventured. "It seems I need a real sword and a long knife. Can you make them for me?"

Fazulo laughed lightly. "Not a problem. What do you want them to look like?"

With his right hand, Angus drew his sword and held it at the ready. The sun striking the blade cast a blinding reflection in the two young men. With his left, he drew the long knife, crossing the two blades at chest high level.

Fazulo reached for the sword. "May I?" he asked.

Angus handed him the weapon.

Fazulo looked at the sword with a trained eye. Carefully, he moved it side to side, and then swung it from back to front. Without touching the blade, he moved his hand carefully along its length, then examined the handle.

"This is some beautiful work," he observed.

"It was made for me," Angus replied proudly.

Respectfully, Fazulo turned the sword and returned it to Angus, hilt first. Angus turned the long knife and passed it to the young man in the same manner.

To Andrew's surprise, Fazulo took even more time and care examining the long knife.

"Light," Fazulo said absently, "but very strong. Probably 420 stainless. Balance is forward." Looking at Angus, he asked, "Do you throw this?"

Angus just smiled.

"Thought so," Fazulo said admiringly. "It's balanced for throwing, and the tip is over-folded to make it stronger. This," he held the knife out to Andrew, "is a work of art."

"Can you make me one like it?" Andrew asked.

"Of course," Fazulo responded. "You may be the Wyatt Earp of the courts, but I'm the Eric Clapton of the machine shop!"

Both young men laughed and bumped knuckles. Angus waited patiently, trusting that they had reached an agreement.

Fazulo returned the knife to Angus with a gentleness that showed his respect for the workmanship. Angus could not help but like the lad, even though he understood nothing of the conversation between Fazulo and Andrew.

Andrew pointed toward the machine shop, indicating that he was ready to return.

"Not yet, Bro," Fazulo said. "If you're really going to use them, which I am pretty sure you are, I need to know a little more before I lay them out."

"What do you need to know?" Andrew asked.

"Strength, range of motion, endurance....They have to be as heavy as you can handle, but light enough for you to use." Fazulo pointed to the car parked a short distance from where they were standing. "Come with me," he said lightly, "and my chariot will take us to the chamber of torture, where I will measure and test until I know more about you than your mother does!"

Angus was concerned about the reference to a chamber of torture, but Andrew seemed to be undisturbed. The two lads headed for the automobile, Angus and Erin following behind.

Twenty minutes later, Angus wanted to kiss the ground as he nearly fell from the automobile. He had never been taken on such a high speed, bumpy, twisty ride in his life. Erin was ecstatic, but Angus was happy to be back on solid ground!

The foursome headed for a building with high windows. It looked much like the gymnasiums where Andrew played basketball.

As they neared the high structure, they shifted direction towards a smaller building attached to the side of the larger one.

The room inside the smaller building was filled with apparatus that were alien to Angus. He recognized nothing except the free weights, which were like the ones Andrew had purchased early in Angus' stay in this strange world. The other machines were a total mystery to the dragonslayer.

Angus and Erin sat while Fazulo connected Andrew to all manner of machines, having him swing his arm, lift weights, bend, and otherwise contort while Fazulo wrote on a pad. When they finished, Andrew asked, "How'd I do?"

"Well," Fazulo laughed, looking at his paper, "other than the fact you're not human, I'd say pretty well."

Andrew and Angus both stared at Fazulo, confused by his response.

"Just for example," Fazulo explained, "you can move your arm every possible direction beyond what most people can reach. But, even more amazing," he added, "you are off-the-charts strong, and you are as strong in any position as you are with your arm straight ahead. It's impossible, but you are like a weight lifter in every position I can put you in. That's also true of your legs, your back...everything. There's some serious ju-ju going on with your bod, Bro. I can measure it, but I can't believe it."

"Can you make the sword and knife?" Andrew asked, ignoring Fazulo's compliments.

"Of course," Fazulo responded as if offended. "And you are going to be one deadly S.O.B. when I do!"

Andrew smiled.

Fazulo walked toward the exit, continuing to look over his paper. Andrew, Angus, and Erin followed. When they reached the car, Angus declined the ride.

"If you don't need me," he said politely to Fazulo, "I'll walk back. I need the exercise, and it's a beautiful day."

"No problem," Fazulo responded. "In fact, I was just going to drop you off at home. I have work to do, but you don't need to be there. It will take about two days to put these together, and then I will bring them to you." Pausing, he added, "I don't want the guys at the shop to see what I'm doing, so I'll be working at night."

Fazulo turned to Andrew. "I'll have them for you by Tuesday night, but you owe me some serious explanation when I deliver them!"

"Cool," Andrew replied. The two young men bumped knuckles, and Andrew walked back to where Angus was standing.

When Fazulo opened the driver's door, Erin jumped in and sat in the passenger seat, tail wagging excitedly.

Fazulo laughed. "I think she wants another ride."

"If you don't mind, that's fine with me," Angus assured him. "She'll find her way home from wherever you go."

Fazulo chuckled under his breath. "Somehow, I thought so," he observed.

On Tuesday evening, Fazulo arrived in time to have dinner with the family. Angus and Erin were happy to be invited. There was no discussion of swords or knives; Charise questioned Fazulo about his employment after college, and he complimented her on her cooking. After dinner, Andrew had suggested they play Dragon's Tale, so Charise and Latisha set about doing dishes as the three men excused themselves. Erin found a corner of the kitchen where she could lay and watch the women clean, hoping for a few table scraps.

Before going to Angus' apartment, the small troop walked out to Fazulo's car and picked up a long canvas bag. Lovingly, Fazulo carried them to Angus' room and lay the package on the table.

Carefully, Fazulo unwound the burlap. As he unwrapped the first two layers, the long knife came into view. It was beautiful, glowing in the artificial light of the kitchen. Lovingly, Fazulo handed it to Andrew, who took it in his left hand and felt its weight and balance. It was the first long knife he had ever held, but he knew immediately it was perfect for him.

As Fazulo started to unwrap further, the doorbell rang. The three men looked at each other, shrugging to indicate they did not know who might be at the door. Andrew slid the long knife between the refrigerator and counter, out of sight from any casual visitor. Angus went to the door.

It was Ayana, dressed in harambe and headscarf. Angus stepped back as Ayana let herself in and walked directly to the kitchen.

Fazulo and Andrew stood back, completely taken by the beauty before them. When Angus reached the kitchen and saw the look on their faces, he smiled. He had not seen that look often, but he knew what it meant...they were smitten, and Ayana could do anything she wanted with no protest from either boy.

Ayana smiled at the young men, and then walked to the table. Carefully, she opened the burlap to expose the sword.

Holding her hand above the sword, she touched the flat of the blade with the tip of her index finger. The light from the end of her nail was as bright as the welders in Fazulo's machine shop. Slowly but surely, she moved as if writing on the sword. When she finished, she stepped back and admired her handiwork. There, on the sword, was script, written with her fingernail into hardened stainless steel as if she were scratching in soft cheese.

Angus stepped up to see what she had done. After a moment, he read aloud, "Andrew, son of Amira, descendant of Solomon and

Sheba through Ebna la-Hakim, legacy of Seth. It's elven script," he told the boys. "This is now Andrew's sword."

"And a fine sword it is," Ayana said admiringly. Looking to Fazulo, she smiled. "Your father, and his father before him, would be proud to see this work of your hands. These weapons do honor to your ancestors, who lived in the mountains and learned their skills from the dwarves. You are a craftsman to be regarded with respect."

Fazulo nearly passed out from the excitement of having such a beauty admire his work.

Delicately, Ayana lifted the sword with both hands, presenting the hilt to Andrew. As he stepped forward and accepted it from her, it began to glow.

"Take your sword, Dragonslayer, and make it your own. From this day forth, it will serve only you. It is the sword of a prince among men, a man of honor and courage. Treat it kindly, for it is as much a part of you as your arm or your heart."

As she spoke, Andrew felt the heat of the sword in his hand. He could feel the power as it surged into the sword and back into his hand. When the sword cooled and the feelings passed, he felt fatigued as never before--yet he also felt strong and ready for anything.

Ayana turned to Angus. "You have done well, Angus the Elder, in preparing Andrew for what lies ahead. When his schooling is done, it will be time for him to return with you to the Land of Dragons."

Angus nodded. "Aye," he replied respectfully, "I will bring him to the field of honor. But I have not yet told the full truth to his mother and the foundling, and I am not sure how they will respond."

Ayana smiled.

"All will be well with the Princess and her charge," she assured him. "She is fond of you, and protective of her son. As for the foundling," she added, "she will go wherever Erin travels, and will rejoice in her adventures."

"Thank you," Angus said with a small bow of his head. "I will speak with them soon."

Ayana stepped forward and kissed the Elder on his forehead. The young men were visibly jealous.

"You are a good man, Angus the Elder," she assured him. "The Land of the Dragons has missed you, and will rejoice with your return."

Turning to the young men, she smiled.

"We will meet again, young prince," she said to Andrew. Looking to Fazulo, she said, "You will remember naught of this adventure, but you will always know that whatever you do will always be of the highest quality. You are blessed," she finished, and Fazulo could almost feel her blessing flow through his body.

Ayana left as silently as she arrived. Andrew wrapped the sword and knife carefully in the burlap, then placed them on top of the refrigerator.

When the men returned to Charise's apartment, she had finished the dishes and had set out cheese cake for each of them. As they sat down, Latisha returned from having taken the trash to the dumpster.

Fazulo arrived at home, full from the meal and happy that he had visited with Andrew's family. The old guy at dinner didn't really fit in with them, but he could tell that Andrew's mom liked the old guy more than a little. Before Fazulo closed his door, the drop-dead-gorgeous girl from across the hall opened hers and smiled at him.

"I have some cake, but I don't dare eat it alone or I'll eat it all," she said jokingly. "Care for a little piece?"

As a matter of fact, he did.

◆◆◆◆

The Quest Begins

Chapter the Tenth

elling Charise was much easier than Angus had anticipated. He waited until they had dinner and both Latisha and Andrew had things to do afterwards. As they sat in the living room after dinner, Angus told her about Ayala and the need to return to the Land of Dragons. Surprisingly, Charise was almost anxious to see the dragons, and she seemed fine with accompanying him.

As Angus explained about the war of the dragons and the returning threat, Charise became more concerned. She asked a long string of questions, but ultimately agreed that it was important that they support the efforts to resist the armies from the east. Angus was amazed at how determined she seemed as she discussed the dangers in matter-of-fact terms. It reminded him of her reaction when they had been attacked on the street; she grasped the risk, but she understood the realities and accepted them.

Angus did not discuss the need for Andrew to face a dragon, and he regretted not having explained it to her. Keeping it from her made him feel uncomfortable, but he didn't know how to address it. When he was leaving and she bent to kiss him on the cheek, his conscious got the best of him.

"There is one other thing I need to explain to you," he said, standing where she could not close the door.

Charise nodded. "I thought so," she remarked. "You're not a very good liar."

"Ayala made it clear that Andrew must face a dragon," he said quietly.

Charise nodded him back into the room. Angus returned to his normal chair.

Charise was silent for several minutes, and Angus waited patiently. He knew it was hard for mothers to accept the dangers of dragonslaying, and he was not sure Charise would be willing to let Andrew face that fate.

Finally, she sighed deeply.

"I don't understand all this," she said finally, "but I feel that it's all connected." Charise paused, searching for the right words. "I want to say no," she admitted, "but I trust you and I trust Andrew. I know how you feel about him, and I believe that you would not put him at risk if you did not believe it was necessary."

Charise's tears hurt Angus more than all the wounds he had endured in ten thousand battles. He didn't know what to do, so he sat quietly and waited. Finally, she drew a deep breath, and said quietly, "Please make sure he's ready."

"Aye," Angus said quietly, standing to go.

Charise stood up and moved to where Angus was standing, putting her arms around him and lay her head on his shoulder. Angus had never had a woman hold him this way, and he wasn't sure what to do, so he put his arms around her and patted her on the back. He wasn't sure where that instinct came from, but Charise was crying on his shoulder and he felt he had to do something.

After several minutes, Charise finished crying. As she drew back her arms and stood up, she kissed Angus on the cheek. Wiping her eyes, she walked to the door. Angus stopped as he walked past her, wanting to say or do something to make her feel better. When he looked up to her face, she bent down and kissed him on the lips.

All the battles and all the training did not keep Angus' heart from racing and his knees from going weak.

Charise pulled away self-consciously. Turning, she went into her apartment and closed the door.

Reluctantly, Angus returned to his quarters.

The next day, Angus and Andrew discussed his training with the sword and long knife. Latisha walked in on the discussion and offered to show them a place where they could practice without being seen. Half an hour later, she let them into the abandoned garage previously used by the Gladiatores. When they agreed the space would work, Latisha left them to their practice.

Angus demonstrated the various movements with the sword, and Andrew followed his instructions carefully. The sword felt natural in his hand, and the moves were quite similar to those he learned in basketball. For an hour, they practiced synchronized movements all around the garage.

As lunch time approached, Ayala appeared at the door of their practice area.

"The moves come naturally to you," she commented to Andrew. "Do they feel as natural as they look?"

Andrew smiled and nodded.

"He will be facing armed men, as well as dragons," she said to Angus. "Perhaps it would be good to practice that."

Angus shook his head.

"I have no wooden swords," he explained, "and these blades are far too deadly to practice with."

Ayana nodded. "I agree. But let me show you an alternative."

Ayana walked to Angus and put her hand on his shoulder. "Feel this. Remember the feeling."

Angus felt a tingle throughout his body, and noticed as it passed through his hand to his sword. Within a minute, the tingle was gone.

"Now, strike me," Ayala said, stepping back.

Angus hesitated.

"Go ahead," she encouraged him. "Trust me."

Angus swung the sword gently, striking Ayala on her arm. There was no blood, no injury at all. When Ayala gave him a critical look, he swung harder and hit her in the same area. Again, not even a bruise.

Ayala smiled. "You can do this as well," she told Angus. "You have more than enough magic to protect yourself and Andrew."

Motioning for Andrew to join them, she instructed Angus, "Place your hand on his shoulder."

Angus complied.

"Now, remember the feeling," Ayala said quietly.

Angus felt the tingle through his hand, and he could see Andrew experiencing the feelings he had felt earlier.

"Now," Ayala instructed as the men finished. "Try it out," she said to Andrew.

Andrew looked concerned, but he raised his sword and looked for something to strike. Ayala held her shoulder to him, and he reluctantly struck her. Again, no blood or bruise.

"You can do this any time you want," she told Angus. "Then you can practice one-on-one without anyone losing an arm."

Angus had to laugh.

"How do I take off the spell?" he asked.

"The same way," Ayala replied. "You'll feel the magic returning through your hand."

"How do I protect myself?" he asked.

"Cross your heart," she replied, placing her right hand over her left and moving them both to her left breast.

Ayala stepped back to the doorway. "Let me see," she instructed.

Angus raised his sword to the ready. Andrew followed suit. When the Elder struck, Andrew blocked easily. As the men repeatedly struck and parried, their speed picked up. Finally, Angus feinted and moved in to strike Andrew on his sword arm.

No blood, no bruise.

Ayala smiled, then waved as she left.

The men continued their practice, sword on sword. As they moved faster and faster, Andrew's skill increased with every strike. Suddenly, they realized Charise was standing at the doorway and both men stopped simultaneously.

The look on Charise's face left both men feeling guilty. She was clearly upset seeing them spar, but she said nothing. Finally, she asked, "Have you seen Latisha?"

"Not since she showed us this garage," Andrew responded. "That was a couple of hours ago. Is there a problem?"

"No," Charise replied, "it's just lunch time. Do you want to eat?"

Both men nodded. "Yes, please," they said, almost in unison.

As the men packed the swords into their cases, Latisha walked up behind Charise.

"There you are," Charise commented.

"I am hungry," Latisha replied. "Is it dinner yet?"

The four walked back to the apartment.

After lunch, Angus and Andrew added long knives to their practice. Using both the sword and the long knife was unnatural at first, but Andrew caught on as he had with the sword. By the end of the day, he moved naturally with the sword, the long knife, and both. Angus was pleased, and Andrew was excited with his new skills.

With no basketball practice to take up his afternoons, Andrew focused on his training with the sword and long knife. He and Angus would run every day, stopping after an hour or so to practice balance and do calisthenics. Then they would run again, and each day Andrew ran farther and faster. Angus was pleased with his progress, but Andrew kept working harder. The thought of facing a dragon was always in the back of Andrew's mind, and he knew the outcome would either be victory or death. The thought of dying was a strong motivator.

Charise was holding up well, under the circumstances. She prepared for her trip to the land of dragons, arranging for another manager to take over the apartment complex and beginning her own fitness program. She initially rejected Angus' offer to run with her, since she felt like she would be holding him back. When she ultimately agreed, the two spent much of each day building her speed, strength and stamina. Charise ended each workout by kissing Angus on the cheek when they separated, and Angus found that he looked forward to those tender moments more and more.

Charise decided that she would tell Latisha about the impending adventure, and it was as Ayala predicted--Lathisha was excited by the prospect of traveling to a new and strange land. When Charise asked Angus and Erin to show Latisha their true images, Latisha was thrilled and kissed Angus on the cheek. When she took Erin's jaw in her hands and kissed her on the head, Angus felt a sense of déjà vu, but couldn't quite place where the feeling came from.

As Andrew completed his final exams and prepared for graduation, the mood changed. Charise felt a sense of loss, since she was leaving behind a life she had become accustomed to over the years, yet she felt excitement at the prospect of seeing the land of dragons. Her fear for Andrew never subsided, though, and she found herself speaking with Angus about it on the day of Andrew's graduation ceremony.

"You know," she said one night as they relaxed after dinner, "Andrew's father was a soldier, and he died in battle." Angus could see her fighting tears as she paused to get her emotions back under control. "Andrew looks just like him." Again, Charise paused, fighting for control. "He died protecting the other men in his squad. There was an ambush, and he stayed behind until all the others could find cover. In the end, his squad managed to kill all the enemy attackers, but by that time he was dead."

Charise held out a ribbon with a medal secured to its end.

"This is what they sent me. I buried him knowing he had died fighting for something he believed in. But I will never believe it was worth his life, or the life of the others who died."

Angus sat silently while Charise cried.

As she again gained control, Charise looked at Angus through bloodshot eyes.

"Please tell me that if I lose my son, it will be a sacrifice for something worthwhile."

Angus struggled to find the right words. He was a dragonslayer, not a philosopher, and he found it hard to express his feelings, especially about someone for whom he cared so deeply.

"I do not know the reasons why we must do what we are about to do," he said softly. "I am a dragonslayer, and I have spent most of my life in battles where the only two outcomes were victory or death. I do not value my life the same way you value Andrew's, but I feel the same as you about the value of his life. I believe what we are about to do is part of something bigger than us, and that it is important for us to take this journey." He paused, seeking the right words. "If I ever begin to doubt the necessity of what we are doing, I will stop and send Andrew back to this world. I have seen hundreds of men die, and I have now learned that those men lost their lives fighting for something that was less than noble. I will not make that mistake with Andrew."

Charise left her chair and sat on Angus' lap, hugging his neck and placing her face into his shoulder. She was not crying, but Angus shared her need for comfort and appreciated her touch as much as she appreciated his. Silently, he mourned the need for this adventure, but he knew in his heart that fate had set him on this path and that he would have to follow it to the end.

After a while, Charise kissed Angus on the cheek and stood, straightening her dress.

"Well," she said, "I guess we need to get ready to go."

The graduation ceremony was long, and Angus could barely see Andrew from their seats in the balcony of the huge auditorium. Afterwards, they celebrated with cake and cola, and Angus was again reminded how much of this strange world he would miss.

At midnight, Angus and Erin returned to their apartment to prepare for the impending departure. At sunrise, they returned to Charise's apartment to gather the three companions.

As they walked eastward from the apartment building, no one spoke. There was a moment's pause when Erin suddenly changed from a beagle into a dragon, and the surroundings changed from houses and streets to a dirt road leading through a small forest. Angus was about to explain the change when Charise resumed the trek along the dirt road. With a flapping of her wings, Erin took to the sky to serve as their airborne scout. Charise took the lead, walking just slightly ahead of Angus, with Latisha following and Andrew bringing up the tail of their formation.

At lunch time, Charise stopped under the shade of an ancient oak and laid out a blanket from her backpack. Within minutes, the four travelers were eating chicken and potato salad as if they had been traveling to this spot for a picnic.

As they finished, Garand arrived and, after introductions, was given his first taste of sweet iced tea. He was surprised at the cold blend of bitter and sweet, but pleased. Everyone but Latisha engaged in light chatter as they all finished their meal.

After the meal was finished and the blanket and food were again stowed in Charise's backpack, they resumed their eastward journey along the road. Just before nightfall, they stood atop a small knoll and saw a village below.

"We will be spending the night here," Garand announced. "I've arranged for rooms at an inn."

Erin landed as Garand finished speaking.

"What about Erin?" Latisha asked.

"Erin will be fine in the countryside," Garand replied.

"I think not!" Latisha retorted. Her tone took the others by surprise. "I think she'll be a dog again for the night, and she can spend it with me!"

After a moment, Garand smiled.

"As you wish," he said as the dragon disappeared and was replaced by a beagle.

At the inn, Garand approached the innkeeper, who led them upstairs to several small rooms. As he pointed out the first one, Latisha and Erin walked in and made themselves at home.

Andrew took the second room, and Garand took the third.

At the fourth room, Charise took Angus' hand and pulled him along as she entered. "I'll feel safer if you are here with me," she said to him, ignoring the innkeeper's knowing look.

"I won't be far," Angus began to protest.

"I know," Charise responded quickly, "but I want you here. Please?"

Angus nodded, and the innkeeper left.

As nightfall arrived, the travelers lit candles, but within an hour the candles had been extinguished and all were sleeping soundly. Erin slept on the floor next to Latisha, and Angus slept on the floor next to Charise. Both women slept at the edge of their beds, arms over the side so they could touch their companion.

••••

Return to the World of Science
Chapter the Eleventh

At daybreak, Angus and Andrew ran through the town and into the hills beyond. They ran along a winding path into the hills, and pushed through the rocky terrain without slowing or stopping. Andrew was amazed at how much stamina he had developed, and was determined to match the old dragonslayer step for step.

At the inn, Charise awakened to find the dragonslayer gone. As she searched the room for her clothes, she found a pile of new garments laying across a chair, under a note that said simply, "Charise".

Slipping into a harambe, Charise found it quite comfortable. It was full of delicate earth toned patterns and was trimmed with a beautiful purple satin-like cloth. Once dressed, she went downstairs to find the innkeeper.

"I would like a bath," she informed him.

"Yes, ma'am," he replied, bowing. "Anastasia!" he shouted at the kitchen. A teenage girl, about the same age as Latisha, rushed out.

"Madam would like a bath!" he commanded.

The girl moved toward the stairs, bowing as she passed Charise. At the second stair she stopped and looked back, waiting for Charise to follow. Thanking the innkeeper, Charise turned and followed the girl.

In the room across from hers, there was a small tub and a large pail of water heating on a stove. The girl poured about half the pail into the tub, then added a half pail of unheated water from another pail in the corner. After stirring the water with her hand, she stepped behind Charise and grasped the collar of her harambe. Charise realized the girl was waiting to help her out of her clothes.

Turning to the girl, Charise said, "That won't be necessary."

The girl looked as if she had been slapped. "Is madam not pleased?" she asked timidly. Charise could tell from the tone of her voice the girl was deeply troubled.

"No, it's fine," Charise replied with a smile. "I can bathe myself."

The girl backed towards the door, looking down as if she was being punished.

"Anastasia," Charise said kindly. "I have always bathed myself, and I am happy to do it here. Why did you think I would need help?"

Anastasia continued to look at the floor. "I've never met a princess before," she replied timidly. "I have always been told the princesses had ladies in waiting, and I was hoping I could serve as yours while you were here."

"What makes you think I am a princess?" Charise asked.

"Madam travels with a sorcerer and is protected by two dragonslayers," came the reply. "Clearly, you are a most important princess."

Charise smiled. After a moment's pause, she turned her back to the girl.

"If you wish to help," she said quietly, "you may."

Anastasia quickly stepped up behind Charise, taking the collar of the harambe as she had before. Charise untied her belt and let the loose garment be removed by the girl.

Stepping into the tub, Charise waited. Quickly, Anastasia used a pan to pour water over her shoulders, wetting her front and back. Soaping a large sponge, the girl handed it to Charise.

When Charise had finished washing her torso and legs, Anastasia washed her back. Setting the sponge aside, Anastasia again poured water over Charise until she had removed all the soap.

Anastasia wrapped Charise in a large towel, and then held her harambe at the ready as Charise dried herself. When Charise stepped out of the tub, Anastasia held the harambe until Charise had wrapped it around herself and tied her belt.

When Charise turned, the girl looked very proud of herself.

"Thank you," Charise said, smiling. "That was most helpful."

Anastasia bowed, and then backed out of the room.

When Charise returned to the first floor, she found Latisha, Erin and Garand sitting at a table eating fruit and drinking hot tea.

"That was an experience," she remarked as she joined them.

After Charise described her experience to Garand and Latisha, Garand smiled.

"These are simple people," he explained, "and they only know what they have been told. They have never seen people of color, so you seem quite exotic to them. Your traveling companions, as well as the purple trim on your clothes, indicate royalty. Since you are actually a princess, they behave as they have been told they should in the presence of royalty."

"But I'm not a princess," Charise corrected him.

Garand looked at her curiously. "Did Angus not tell you about your heritage?" he asked.

"What heritage?" Charise asked.

Garand repeated the information Ayala had conveyed to him and Angus in their meeting at the meadow. Charise listened intently, and then shook her head.

"I'm not sure I believe all that," she observed.

"I'm pretty sure it's true," Garand assured her. "Ayala demonstrated some powerful magic, and she was very serious about your heritage and that of your son. I don't believe she would have lied about all that, and, if she had, I believe I would have detected her deceit."

Charise let out a small laugh. "Is that why you provided me with clothes that are trimmed in purple?" she asked the old sorcerer.

"I didn't provide you with any clothes," he said. His face clearly showed confusion. "What kind of clothes were you provided?"

"This dress and three more like it," she replied. "They are all different colors and patterns, but they are all trimmed in purple."

The sorcerer smiled and shook his head. "I don't know where they came from," he said, smiling, "but they were clearly meant for you."

There was little more conversation as the three ate breakfast. Charise and Garand were lost in their own thoughts, while Latisha petted Erin between bites.

Angus and Andrew returned from their run and joined the others at the table. Andrew was starving, so he asked for some meat to go with the bread and fruit. The innkeeper quickly provided large cuts of ham and fresh bread for the dragonslayers.

As the men ate, Garand provided the information he had gathered since his last meeting with Angus. "The warlords from the East have sent out search parties looking for the Orb of Solomon. In the meantime, they are gathering their troops to our East and preparing for an attack through the mountain pass just south of the dragon breeding grounds," he explained. "They have not been successful yet at finding the Orb, but there are rumors that one group believes they are on the right track.

"The most likely group is in Andrew's world at a place known as Machu Picchu, in a time at the beginning of the twentieth century."

Looking at Andrew, he asked, "Do you know this place?"

Andrew nodded. "It is an ancient Inca pyramid, on top of a mountain in Peru."

"That would be the place," Garand agreed. "Can you visualize this place?"

"Yes," Andrew replied. "I did a report on it in college, so I remember many of the pictures from my references."

"Good," Garand concluded. "You will go to the West and South, then, and keep those images in your mind. Try to focus on the time, as well, because it is important that you arrive at the same place and time as the search party."

"So all I have to do is think of the place and I will go there?" Andrew asked.

Garand laughed. "Welcome to the world of magic, young man. Here we travel until we arrive, and we arrive at the destination we see in our mind. Distance and time are important in your world, but they are meaningless here."

Andrew shook his head in disbelief.

"You will need two horses to ride, and one for provisions," the old sorcerer thought out loud. "Provisions for at least a week, and you should probably wear your armor, just in case you come across the party searching for the Orb."

As the old man finished, Charise corrected, "That will be three horses, plus the pack animal."

Everyone looked at her simultaneously. Charise's face showed her determination. "I will be going with them."

Each of the men began to say something, but the look on Charise's face stopped them before they began. With a sigh, Garand conceded, "Three horses, then."

"Can I stay here?" Latisha asked. "I'm not excited about bouncing around on a horse and sleeping in a tent."

All eyes turned to Charise.

"I would like it if you would stay here," Charise told her. Looking at Angus, she asked, "Will she be safe?"

Angus smiled. "If Erin stays with her, she will be much safer than any of us. But dragons need to eat, and that requires that she leave here to hunt, so I'll arrange for some human protection as well."

Everyone nodded agreement, and Angus rose from his chair. Andrew and Garand rose at the same time, prepared to follow the Elder.

Placing his hand on Charise' shoulder, Angus handed her his purse, now heavy with gold coins. "Take this," he said quietly. "We will need food for a week's travel. If it takes longer, I can supplement with game and we can usually find fresh water along the way."

Charise nodded.

The men left, searching for horses and camp gear for the trip. After the men left, Latisha and Charise headed into the village to buy provisions.

It was nearly dark before everyone arrived back at the inn. The horses were stabled, and the pack saddle was brought inside to prepare it for departure. Angus was proud of how well Charise had chosen their provisions. She had bought meat that would keep along the trail and pack closely with minimal bulk; fruit and vegetables that kept well and did not bruise easily; and bread wrapped in waxed skins to keep it fresh and dry for several days. Charise watched the old dragonslayer with pride as he expertly packed the provisions and camping gear onto the pack saddle.

Ian, a young dragonslayer with green armor, had returned to the Inn with the other men. He was introduced to Charise, then Latisha. He was charged with Latisha's safety while the others were away, and his face could not hide his pleasure when he first laid eyes on the beautiful young girl. Erin placed herself between the young people as they exchanged pleasantries and got to know each other. As the evening drew to a close, Charise looked at the young man and smiled.

"Ian," she said pleasantly, "Did we tell you Erin is actually a dragon?"

The shock was obvious on the young man's face.

"Aye," Angus added, "A fine green scale dragon. And she loves the lass like she was her own baby."

"So," Charise closed the conversation, "between you and the dragon, I believe my baby will be safe. Is that so?"

"Yes, ma'am," Ian assured her.

"Good."

Charise took Angus by the hand and headed up the stairs. The remainder of the troop followed, with Erin between Latisha and Ian.

Everyone arrived in the dining room at sunrise. After a hearty breakfast, Angus and Andrew carried the pack saddle to the stables and prepared the horses.

Erin kept her place between Ian and Latisha, using her head to push the young man's foot away when it strayed too close to Latisha's leg.

Garand took his leave, heading east to find out what he could of the gathering Army.

Charise had a short, but pointed, talk with Latisha before joining the dragonslayers in the stables. She could see the mutual attraction between the young people and reminded Latisha that she was responsible for her actions, even in this strange land. Latisha assured her all would be well.

When she arrived at the stable, Charise' troubled look was immediately noticed by Angus. Sensing what was wrong, he assured her, "Ian is a dragonslayer, and he will protect Latisha with his life."

"It's not her life I'm concerned about at the moment," Charise commented absently, "and I'm not so sure it's *her* that needs protection."

Angus and Andrew looked at each other and shrugged. Neither understood what Charise was saying, but neither wanted to ask any more questions. They finished with the horses without further conversation.

After a proper goodbye, the three travelers set out to the southwest to find the land of the Incas. Latisha, Ian, and Erin watched them leave, and then headed into the village to find distractions for the day.

After their midday meal, the three travelers followed a river through a valley. As they moved forward, the northern forest of hardwood and pine gave way to a tropical forest, pressing ever closer to the river. Angus looked at Andrew, who nodded and said, "This is it."

The road became a trail, and then the trail gave way to a rocky riverbank twisting along to the South. The horses picked their way along the river bank until just before nightfall, when the group found a large cave in which to make camp for the evening.

While the men unsaddled and groomed the horses, Charise went into the cave to build a fire and prepare a meal.

As the pack horse was unsaddled, Charise returned to the mouth of the cave and took Angus by the sleeve.

"You need to see this," she said quietly.

Both men followed closely as she walked into the cave toward the rear, where the cave narrowed to a meter or so wide and a few meters tall.

Charise walked into the narrow passageway, holding a lantern for light. Within a few minutes, they walked into another chamber, large enough that the lantern light could not reach the top or the other side.

As all three stood at the entrance to the cathedral chamber, Charise pointed.

Around the floor of the cathedral chamber were small circles of rocks, darkened inside the circle. Each circle was a fire pit, and there were ten or more circles which could be seen from where they stood.

Angus walked into the chamber and directly to one of the fire pits. Feeling the ashes inside the circle, he looked around. He could see animal bones and waxed skins discarded on the floor around the fire pit. Walking to a pile of refuse, he picked up a waxed skin, exactly like the ones they used to carry bread.

Holding the skin up for Charise and Andrew to see, he said, "It seems we have found the camp of the search party."

The sound of horse hooves caused all three to look at the far end of the cave. In the dim light, they could barely make out a larger tunnel entrance. Angus returned the skin to its original position, and then walked quickly to Andrew and Charise.

"Douse the light," he whispered the Charise. He led them back into the passage from whence they had come, stopping a few yards in and hiding in the shadow of an outcropping rock.

The three watched as twenty or more soldiers, wearing the battle gear of the eastern army, entered the chamber. Clearly, the soldiers did not sense their presence, for they set about building fires and preparing to settle in for the evening.

After an hour of watching the soldiers, Angus motioned for Andrew and Charise to follow him. They moved quietly to the opening of the cave, then outside to the river. Darkness had come to the river, and not a single star offered its light to the travelers.

"So, what do we do now?" Charise whispered.

"We can't stay here," Angus replied. "If one of them comes through our tunnel looking for a place to relieve his bladder, we will be found out."

"Well, we can't go up or down the river," Charise argued. "It's darker here than it is in the cave. The horses will never be able to find footing in this dark, and we'll all wind up crocodile bait if we fall in."

Even Angus knew what a crocodile was, and had to agree it would not be good to travel the river at night.

Andrew spoke quietly. "Mom," he said, looking to Charise, "you go half way down the tunnel and listen, in case someone comes this direction. Angus and I will saddle the horses in case we have to leave. Then I'll go a little further up the tunnel, protecting us from the front. Angus can protect from the rear." When he sensed agreement from his mother and the old dragonslayer, Andrew added, "We'll all try not to fall asleep until they leave in the morning. And if we can't stay awake until then, just pray we don't snore!"

In spite of the danger, both Charise and Angus chuckled under their breath. Then, quietly, each of them set about executing Andrew's plan.

◆◆◆◆

Machu Picchu

Chapter the Twelfth

All went well through most of the night, as Andrew stood watch in the front of the passageway and Angus watched from the rear. Andrew thought it would be hard to stay awake after a long day of traveling, but mortal fear was a great motivator.

At some point, one of the men started down the passage toward Andrew, but he stopped after a few feet and relieved himself on the wall. Andrew held his breath until the man returned to his blanket and lay down.

It was just before sunrise before the next soldier started down the passage. He stopped short of where Andrew stood, acting as if he were going to relieve himself as the other man had done. Then he looked up as if he heard something, raising his nose to the air and sniffing.

As Andrew held his breath, he heard one of the horses snort.

Andrew's vision had become accustomed to the very low light in the passage, and he could see, with the firelight from the cavern behind him, that the man was turning toward him. Andrew's sword was in his hand, even though he could not remember taking it from its scabbard. When the man stepped cautiously toward him, Andrew's heart raced.

This was what they had feared--if one soldier found them, the others would rouse and there would be twenty to follow the first. Andrew considered retreating, waiting to see if the man stopped, but he knew in his heart the man would follow the sound of the horses and would find him, his mother, and Angus as well. Various scenarios played out in his head at a blinding speed, and only one had a chance--attack and hope the soldiers could be routed by the surprise.

Andrew waited until he could hear the soldier's raspy breathing before stepping out from behind the outcropping that had concealed him.

"Hello," Andrew said simply, reaching forward with his sword and using the tip to cut the belt on the man's trousers.

Turning to run, the man's trousers fell to his ankles and he tumbled forward. His scream of pain, as he hit the stone floor of the tunnel, was loud enough to wake the dead, vibrating through the tunnel and echoing in the cavern beyond.

Andrew slapped the man on his behind with the flat of his sword, and the man jumped to his feet, pulling his trousers up and running awkwardly toward the cavern.

Andrew followed the soldier, racing into the cavern with sword and long knife drawn. As the roused soldiers tried to move from sleep to fighting, he moved quickly through them, cutting their lances with his sword and screaming at the top of his lungs.

Having run all the way through the soldiers to the far side, Andrew turned for the real fight. Several men stood with swords out, waiting for his next move.

Andrew walked back into the men, ready for his first real fight.

The first man raised his sword and swung it at Andrew, waist high, like a baseball bat. Andrew struck down with his sword, hitting the flat of the man's sword just ahead of the hilt. Andrew's tempered stainless blade cut right through the man's sword, and the blade bounced noisily across the rocks of the floor.

The second man raised his sword over his head, and Andrew sliced across it. The dismembered blade fell straight down, hitting the man on his head and slicing his scalp as it fell to the ground.

Andrew picked up speed, moving through the group. Now that he knew his sword would cut or break the swords of the soldiers, he moved quickly to cut the swords across their flat side and make them useless to the soldiers.

By the time Andrew reached the tunnel from which he had emerged, a dozen swords and at least that many lances had been sliced in two by his sword and knife.

The soldiers were in full retreat. Several knocked over their comrades as they ran to the opening on the far side of the cavern. Andrew watched in disbelief, amazed that so much chaos could be caused by running and screaming through the crowd.

As the first soldier ran to the tunnel through which they had entered the cavern, a glow came from just inside it. Andrew shaded his eyes as the glow became beacon-bright, and it moved into the cavern.

From behind the glow came a voice he recognized--Ayala!

"Run, fools!" she said in a voice that echoed through the chamber. "Run from Prince Andrew, descendent of Solomon and Sheba, legacy of Seth, and dragonslayer in the service of Angus, Slayer of Garth! Return to your lords, and tell them what you have seen. Tell your lords that they can send one hundred soldiers, or one hundred times one hundred, and they will all perish at Andrew's sword! There is no orb here; only death on the blade of the great Prince!"

The soldiers were all on their knees, bowing to the light and the voice.

"Now, Run!" Ayala commanded, and the light disappeared. The soldiers looked up as the darkness descended on them, then jumped to their feet and ran out of the cavern.

Andrew watched the chaotic retreat, and then heard movement behind him. With his sword still out, he turned.

Ayala smiled, and he could see her in the darkness as if it were day. Her presence emitted a glow that was warm and pleasing, providing perfect illumination. He was smitten, as he had been the first time they met in Angus' kitchen.

"Excellent plan, Andrew," she said with a smile. "There could have been much bloodshed, though, so perhaps you will think things through a little more in your next confrontation."

Angus and Charise came up from behind Ayala, and she turned to let them pass.

Angus made the introductions. "Ayala, Charise. Charise, Ayala." He then stepped past the women to see the carnage left behind by the soldiers. Amid the severed swords and lances were clothes, food, and perfectly serviceable weapons that had been abandoned by the soldiers.

Angus patted Andrew on the back. "Sometimes," he remarked, "the worst plan turns out to bring the best results."

Andrew turned to the old dragonslayer, who was laughing.

"I think it was a pretty good plan," he insisted.

"Lad," Angus said, "if you have to fight against bad odds, the tighter the quarters the more chance you have. Close quarters, such as that tunnel, denies the enemy the advantage of numbers. In the tunnel, you can slice them up one or two at a time and the stack of dead bodies works to keep the others at bay. Running into an open room with twenty-odd armed men gives them the advantage."

Shaking his head, he returned to Charise and Ayana.

"Not a drop of blood was shed," he reassured Charise, "neither by Andrew, nor by the soldiers. Everyone lives to fight another day."

"Hey!" Andrew retorted angrily. "When I snapped that guy's sword over his head, it sliced his scalp pretty good!"

"My mistake," Angus smiled. "Very little blood was shed."

Andrew was still visibly angry. Angus walked back over to him.

"Lad," he said consolingly, "when I say no blood was shed, it's a compliment. I have seen you use that sword, and you could have butchered them like pigs at the packing house. But you found another way, and emerged victorious with your soul intact." The old dragonslayer paused. "I'm proud of you for finding a solution that did not cost the lives of anyone."

Andrew walked away, down the tunnel toward their horses. Angus followed, taking Charise by the hand as he passed. Ayala waved goodbye, and both Angus and Charise waved back. By the time they reached the cave at the end of the tunnel, morning light illuminated their way.

Andrew sat on a stone at the mouth of the cave, deep in thought. Angus walked over to where he was.

"What bothers you, Lad?" he asked Andrew.

Andrew looked up. His mother stood behind Angus, and he could see the concern on both their faces.

"Did you see me run into the cavern?" he asked Angus.

"Aye," the old dragonslayer replied, "I was there within a moment."

"Why didn't you come to help me?" Andrew challenged.

"I am your teacher," Angus said quietly, "not your comrade. I can teach you the way of the sword and knife, how to use the lance, and how to take the measure of your opponent. But I cannot fight for you. If I were to come to your aid, it would mean I lack faith in your abilities, and that is not the case. You are more than able to deal with those men, and you did. I will not take that away from you by interfering."

Andrew looked doubtful. Silently, he stood and walked past his teacher and his mother, and began preparing the horses for the day's journey.

As Angus turned, Charise was still standing between him and Andrew.

"What if he had died in there?" she asked.

"Then I would have killed them all, and mourned his death for the rest of my days," the old man replied sadly.

Silently, they walked together to help Andrew.

As they prepared to mount, Ayala exited the mouth of the cave.

"Follow the river until it forks," she said, "then leave your horses and cut your way up the hill, through the jungle. At the top, you will find the pyramid of the Inca. Andrew must reach the top of the pyramid in time to stand in the light of the setting sun. There is a temple at the top, and he must enter the temple and stand in the last light. If he does this, he will see great visions and will know the next step in his journey."

Ayala turned and returned to the cave without a wave.

The three riders mounted. Angus took the reins of the pack horse. Looking to Andrew, he said, "You heard her, Lad. Let's go."

Andrew reined his horse to the south, along the river bank.

The riders reached the fork of the river by noon. Andrew and Angus groomed and tethered the horses and pitched camp. By the time the camp was completed, Charise had prepared a lunch with meat, cheese, bread and ale. The three ate in silence, looking at the jungle leading up the mountain.

After lunch, Andrew stood.

"I guess I'd best be going," he announced, "if I'm going to stand in the last light."

Angus and Charise stood, but Andrew held his hand out to stop them.

"I will move fastest on my own," he said. "I can use my long knife to cut through the jungle, but I'll never make it in time if I have to wait for either of you. This is something I need to do on my own."

Charise and Angus stood as Andrew picked his way across the river, stepping from boulder to boulder. On the other side, he waved at them before beginning to hack his way through the jungle. Within minutes, he was out of sight.

Andrew moved as quickly as he could, cutting vines and jumping over low scrub on a nearly vertical hillside. At times, he was pulling himself up using tree limbs and vines, because of the steepness of the mountain. As the air grew thinner and the climb grew longer, he found himself fighting for breath in a way he had almost forgotten. Even as his muscles strained on the climb, he realized he would have had no chance of completing this task if he had not been training for years with the old dragonslayer.

As suddenly as it had begun, the jungle ended. Andrew looked up, and could see the steps of Machu Picchu. Leaving the jungle, he moved up a trail leading to the steps of the pyramid. Once clear of the canopy, he looked behind him and could see the sun sinking low toward the horizon.

Quick calculations told him he had but minutes to reach the top of the pyramid, if he was to stand in the last light. As his lungs screamed, Andrew broke into a run and sprinted to the base of the steps.

Andrew did not slow down as he reached the steps of the pyramid. Step by step, he raced up the western slope. His lungs screamed for oxygen, as did his leg muscles, but he pushed on as the sun dropped faster and faster toward the horizon.

Finally, he reached the top of the pyramid and sprinted to the temple.

Inside, Andrew could see the last light as it shone in a six inch vertical line on the eastern wall of the temple. Without thinking, he sprinted as the line became shorter and shorter.

The line was a mere two inches long when he reached the back wall. Facing west, he fell to his knees, the light reflecting off his green armor.

Andrew closed his eyes.

Suddenly, it was as if he were standing atop a mountain, looking out over an army with tens of thousands of soldiers. The sky was dark with dragons, all red and flying in circles as they approached him. Andrew knew the army was that of his enemy, and the dragons would be attacking first.

Andrew shook with fear as he looked out over the Army. They were coming for him, and he would feel the first blood of a battle that would decide the fate of many.

As the fear reached its peak, Andrew felt the weight of the world on his shoulders. He knew he could run fast enough and far enough to get away, leaving the fight to someone else. There was no reason for him to fight; this was not his world, and the people around him were not his people.

As the thought of retreat pushed harder on his mind, Andrew felt a calm pushing from another part of his soul. He would stand and fight, dying if that was what it took. He could not flee, for fleeing was not in his nature. He had a final image of the old dragonslayer, standing alone in a field facing the ultimate adversary, the turquoise dragon that had sent thousands to their fate in its fire. He was a dragonslayer, like Angus the Elder, and he would face the fire, from whatever source, and either win or die; no other fate would do.

Suddenly, the fear was gone and the image of the army and its dragons was clearer, more distinct. He could see the patterns of their formations; feel their movements, as they walked into the rocks and had to break formation to move through the tight confines of the pass. He could see the dragons circling, fighting the mountain's updrafts as they sought to attack. Yes, there were weaknesses. And dragonslayers knew how to take advantage of weaknesses.

When Andrew opened his eyes, the sun was gone, yet his armor still emitted a green luminescence. He was a dragonslayer, and he would fight to the end.

But, for now, he would sleep-after two long days and one long night, he would finally sleep.

Andrew lay on the floor of the temple, flat against the cold floor. Closing his eyes, he slept and dreamed of dragons--not the red battle dragons of the east, but the beautiful green dragons that lived in the provinces.

Back at camp, Angus and Charise spent the evening looking silently at the mountain that Andrew had claimed. As the sun set, Angus felt a sense of peace, and he knew Andrew had made it.

"The lad will be fine," he quietly reassured Charise, who was holding tightly to his right arm and had laid her head on his right shoulder.

"I know," she replied quietly.

Silently, they retreated to their tent and slept, Angus cuddled up behind Charise, his arm over her shoulders.

◆◆◆◆

Return to the Land of Dragons

Chapter the Thirteenth

By the time Andrew returned from the mountain, Charise and Angus had broken camp and saddled the mounts. Andrew hugged his mother, and then slapped Angus' shoulder.

"Leaving without me?" he asked.

Angus smile. "Not yet," he replied lightly.

"Can we go home now?" Charise asked.

Angus looked to Andrew for the answer.

"I think so," Andrew responded. "I can tell you about my visit to the temple as we ride. But I think I got what we came for."

Angus nodded, and then swung onto his mount with practiced ease. Andrew and Charise followed suit. When Angus had the reins of the pack horse, Andrew turned his mount and headed back the way they came, along the stream.

"Do you think we'll run across the soldiers on our way back?" she asked, directing the question to either man.

"I don't," Andrew replied. "They were scared to death by Ayala, and I suspect they headed home as soon as they got out of their cave!"

"Aye," Angus agreed. "But it never hurts to be careful. Keep a good eye out, Lad, and be prepared."

Andrew's prediction proved to be accurate. Just after mid-day, tropical trees and vines gave way to northern pine and live oak.

Andrew had described his vision at Machu Picchu to Angus and his mother. They had few questions, and no one ventured an interpretation. After his description, Andrew fell silent for the rest of the ride, silent in his thoughts of dragons and soldiers.

As they approached the village, Angus spoke. "I think the vision is best kept among us," he ventured. "I'm not sure what is going on here, but I believe the less we share with others the better."

"Including Garand?" Charise asked.

"Aye," Angus replied.

At nightfall, the three rode into the village. As they pulled up in front of their inn, two young boys came out to take the horses. Angus dismounted the supply packs and let the boys take all four animals to the stables.

Charise headed upstairs, Anastasia in tow, to clean up and change clothes. The innkeeper's young daughter seemed to relish her new job as lady-in-waiting, and Charise let her help because it made the girl so happy.

Angus and Andrew wanted dinner worse than they wanted a bath, so they sat at a table with Garand. Over turkey legs and potatoes, they described their encounter with the twenty-odd soldiers in the caves. Garand seemed quite interested, asking questions and speculating on their mission and the reaction to Ayala's dramatic warning.

Neither Angus nor Andrew mentioned the trip to Machu Picchu.

After dinner, Angus left to verify that the horses had been attended to. Garand excused himself, leaving Andrew alone. Within minutes, three young women had joined him at his table, sitting inappropriately close and pouring ale as quickly as he could drink it.

Andrew, who had never been much of a ladies' man, was enjoying the attention.

Within the hour, Andrew was drunk for the first time in his life.

Angus walked into the front door of the inn just in time to catch Andrew being led upstairs by one of the women.

"Whoa, Lassie!" Angus laughed, as she was pushing Andrew up the first step.

The girl looked annoyed as Angus stepped up to take Andrew's weight from the girl. The other girls moved quickly to join their friend.

"Not tonight, I'm afraid," Angus told the girls. "He has yet to slay his first dragon, so he's not ready to entertain." When the girls looked disappointed, he added, "But soon he will be ready, and I'm sure he will remember you fondly."

With practiced precision, Angus spun Andrew and caught the boy across his right shoulder. Waving to the girls, Angus mounted the stairs. Andrew was protesting throughout the climb, but he passed out as soon as Angus laid him on his cot.

Charise was waiting for Angus as he returned to her room.

"What was that all about?" she asked.

"Just some girls wanting to take advantage of our Andrew," he said lightly. "It's not his time yet, so I rescued him and sent them away for now."

Charise looked puzzled. "What do you mean, 'it's not his time yet'?"

"The lad may have the magic and the green armor of a dragon-slayer," Angus explained, "but he has not yet slain a dragon. Until he does, he must leave the lassies alone. If he slays a dragon, then he will forever be the companion of many but the mate of none. If he chooses not to slay the dragon, he can still choose a mate and have a family."

Charise did not understand the old dragonslayer's explanation. Angus had her sit on the bed, while he sat in a chair explaining about the training of dragonslayers and the choice they faced when their training was complete.

"In fact," he concluded, "I have three novices who need to go to the breeding grounds and then to the field of honor. I am sure many will be gathered there, waiting for Andrew to face his first live dragon."

Charise looked shocked. "So the choice Andrew faces is to be a dragonslayer and live with no family or children until he is killed by a dragon. Or he has to walk away from it all and never know whether he could have been a dragonslayer?"

"Aye," Angus nodded.

As the moments went by in silence, Angus became troubled.

"Charise," he said quietly, waiting for her to look up. When she faced him, he could see she had been crying silently. "What I have told you has been true since before I was born, and I have seen many, many summers. But when I met with Ayala and Garand, I learned that much of what I believed to be true was, in fact, just the fabrication of the sorcerers."

Pausing, he added, "Before we mourn the lad's fate, let us wait and see how much more of what I have thought to be true is, in fact, not."

Rising, he moved to the bed and sat beside Charise, holding her close.

Andrew awoke to a terrific hangover. He was still in his traveling clothes, armor and all. He went down the hall to the room with the tub and water, and the bath cleared his head as well as cleaning his body.

When he arrived at breakfast, Andrew was surprised to see his mother, sister, Garand, Ian and Erin, but no Angus.

"Where's Angus?" he asked, sitting with the others.

"He had a group of young dragonslayers to train," Garand answered. Charise shot an angry look at him, but Garand either did not notice or did not care. "He is taking three young dragonslayers to the dragon breeding grounds to let them take the measure of their opponents. Then they will return to the field of valor, where they will face their first dragons."

Andrew was intrigued.

"Is that where I will face my dragon?" he asked.

"Yes. In a few days, we will journey to the central provinces, where we will join Angus and his lads. There, you will face your dragon."

Erin, in her beagle form, whimpered. Latisha reached down and petted her.

Charise stood suddenly and excused herself. She had barely touched her breakfast, and Andrew could see she was upset. As he rose to follow her, his sister motioned for him to stay seated.

Latisha left the table, following her mother. Erin remained, uncharacteristically quiet.

Latisha knocked lightly at her mother's open door. Charise was sitting on the edge of the bed, motionless, looking at the floor. After a respectful pause, Latisha joined her mother, placing her arm around Charise's shoulders.

The two women sat silently, tears running down Charise's face while Latisha held her and stroked the side of her arm. When Charise began to sniffle, Latisha produced a hanky from the sleeve of her dress.

Finally, Charise spoke, still looking at the floor. "When Andrew's father went away," she began softly, "I knew he was doing what he felt was right. There was a war, and he was a soldier, so that's what always happened. I cried myself to sleep every night, worrying about him. Then, when he was killed, I became so angry at him for leaving, that I set about creating a life that was just about me and Andrew. I never mourned my husband; I just moved on without him. He left, and no matter how much of a hero he was to everyone else, he was just the husband that left me, as far as I was concerned.

"Then you came along," Charise added, looking up and smiling. "You helped me fill the void left by a husband that was no longer there. Eventually, I forgave him and moved on.

"Now my son is going to face a dragon, and I'm right back where I started 21 years ago. I don't want him to go, but I can't stop him. I am terrified..." Charise choked back the tears that wanted to resume. "..but I don't know how to stop this."

Latisha kissed her foster mother on the cheek. The cheeks were salty from her tears, but new tears were no longer flowing.

"It will be fine," she told her mother. "Andrew is well prepared, and he will do what needs to be done." After a short pause, she added, "Is Andrew the only one you are crying over?"

Charise looked up. In a moment, she realized the little foundling she had taken in had grown into a beautiful and sensitive woman. Her heart ached for her son, but Latisha had recognized something else. Charise missed Angus, who had been her friend now for nearly six years. More than that, he had been her companion for much of that time, and for the last year had been with her every day.

Charise suddenly realized that Angus' departure had triggered feelings she had not known for a very long time.

"Oh, God!" she said under her breath. "I've fallen in love with a white man who is probably a hundred years older than me!"

Latisha laughed.

Charise laughed, shaking her head.

"He is charming…" Latisha offered, but the look on her mother's face when she said it made her laugh hysterically.

The two women were laughing together when Andrew knocked on the door. Charise, struggling to regain her composure, motioned for him to come in.

"Are you OK?" he asked, looking from his mother to his sister and then back again.

"Yes," Charise smiled. "I just needed to get some things out of my system."

"Ian and I are going to the edge of town to practice with our swords," Andrew ventured. "He has some wooden ones, so I won't need Angus' spell to keep him from cutting off my arm."

"Fine," Charise said. "We'll be OK."

"Erin is out hunting," Andrew added. "Would you prefer that we wait until she's back?"

"We'll be fine," Charise said firmly. "Just be careful."

"OK," Andrew said, kissing his mother's cheek as he prepared to depart. The salty taste of the kiss surprised him, but the look on his mother's face kept him from asking about it.

Charise filled the rest of her morning with odd chores, bathing and then rearranging her room. Angus had rolled his sleeping bag and placed it on the floor at the end of her bed. When she picked it up to place it on a shelf, she found herself hugging the rolled bag and smelling it, catching the unique scent of the old dragonslayer. Realizing what she was doing, she placed it on the shelf next to the window and turned to other chores.

After lunch, she invited Latisha to go for a walk. Andrew and Ian were still gone, and Erin had not returned, so the women set out together.

It was a beautiful day, so Charise headed toward the edge of town. There were a number of meadows along the road into town, and it seemed like a good day to spend enjoying nature.

About a mile out of town, Latisha and Charise stopped to rest on some boulders alongside the road. To their front was a beautiful meadow, full of hay and wildflowers, with an ancient yew tree in its center. To their rear, a hillside full of boulders with flowering vines and scrub trees provided a contrast to the meadow. The day was cool, so the sunshine in their faces felt good to the women.

After resting a few minutes, Charise began to feel uneasy. She had the feeling that someone was behind her, but she dared not look back. Glancing at Latisha, she could see the girl was also uneasy. Without a word, the two women stood and walked across the road before looking back.

There were three men standing on the hillside. They were dressed in oriental style uniforms, carrying swords and shields.

Charise was about to speak with she saw other soldiers stand up, revealing themselves from behind the rocks.

Latisha reached inside her dress and pulled out a sword. It was identical to the one carried by Andrew, Ian, and Angus, but slightly shorter and lighter. Flipping it deftly, she held the sword out to her mother, handle-first.

When Charise took the sword, she felt electric charges shooting up her arm, across her shoulders, and down the other arm. The sword felt like an extension of her arm, and she was ready to use it.

Latisha had drawn another sword, and she was holding it at the ready.

As the men came down the hill toward them, both women raised their swords. The men in front drew their swords, smiling as they moved closer.

When the first two men fell to the women's swords, there was a moment of hesitation among the others. Then, as a mass, the men moved forward. There were no longer any smiles, and the shields were up--they would not underestimate these women as their dead comrades had.

Charise felt as if she were watching herself from another place. She had never trained with a sword, but she was moving as smoothly and strongly as she had seen Andrew and Angus move during practice. She was covered in blood, but it was all from the men who kept coming off the mountain to attack her. In the corner of her eye, she could see Latisha slashing and stabbing as the men piled up at her feet.

No matter how the women fought, they were incredibly outnumbered by the men. There were easily a hundred men coming down that hillside, and the women were fighting in the open. The odds were impossible, but Charise knew she would fight to the end--there was no room here to bargain.

Without warning, there was an ear-shattering scream from the sky, followed by another. Charise glanced up and saw Erin and another bright green dragon diving toward them.

Diving from behind the women, the two dragons sprayed flames up the hillside to the very back of the mass of men. Erin and her mother had been hunting together, and her mother was just about to break off and head home when Erin sighted Latisha and Charise being attacked.

As the dragons finished the first pass up the hillside, they broke away from each other to make a high speed turn. Erin cut off the men trying to escape to Charise's right, while her mother cut off the men on the left. Men were bursting into flames, running in every direction, trying to escape the dragons. Meanwhile, the dragons were cutting off their every escape path, making repeated passes along the edges and back of the formation.

Suddenly, Andrew and Ian came running down the road from town. They had seen the dragon fire and ran as fast as they could to see what the problem was. When they saw the women battling the army of men, they charged even faster, swords and long knives drawn.

It felt like hours, but the battle was actually over within minutes. As the dragons landed, Ian and Andrew began searching through the hundred-plus bodies scattered from the road to the hilltop, looking for any survivors. They wanted to know where these men had come from, who had sent them, what their mission was--anything that could explain such a mass attack on two women.

Only one man, burned from the dragon fire and gasping for breath, could be found alive.

Andrew questioned the man, who shook his head, not understanding what Andrew was saying. As Andrew and Ian began to realize the futility of questioning the soldier in a language he did not know, Latisha pushed between them and took the man's head gently in her hand.

No one understood the words spoken by Latisha except the wounded soldier. As she spoke, he responded. He seemed to feel less pain as she held his head, and he showed his gratitude by babbling for several minutes as Latisha nodded. When he finished, Latisha spoke softly to him as she laid her other hand on his face, closing his eyes with her fingertips. The man relaxed, then his breathing stopped. Latisha laid his head gently on the rocky soil.

"They are what we would call Special Forces," she said to the others, standing over the dead soldier. "They were sent to destroy this town and kill everyone who lives or is visiting there. It's a terror tactic used by their military commanders."

Looking to Erin, Latisha said softly, "There is another group, somewhere between here and the breeding grounds, with the same mission. Can you find them for me?"

Erin took two steps back and extended her wings fully. With a great flapping of wings, she took to the air. Erin's mother looked to Latisha, who nodded; the older dragon stayed close.

Looking to Ian, Latisha said, "We will need all the dragonslayers you can rouse. We don't yet know where, but it will be between here and the breeding grounds. I'll send Erin to find you as soon as she knows where they are."

Ian turned and ran back toward the village. Charise and Andrew stood, staring at the young woman.

"OK," Latisha said finally, "I owe you an explanation. But I don't want to stand here smelling the burnt bodies. Let's go to town and get a burial party formed up to take care of all this."

When she turned, Andrew and Charise followed. Charise was still holding her bloody sword in her right hand.

When they arrived in town, Latisha set about having a group of men sent out to clean up the carnage at the meadow. The men were initially hesitant to go, but Latisha sent Erin's mother to provide security for the men. Satisfied with the security measures, the men set out to build funeral pyres and clean up the field.

In the inn, the first order of business was to get out of the bloody clothes and clean their swords. Andrew's armor cleaned with just a spray of water, and he changed into clean clothes after rinsing the blood off his face, hands and arms.

Anastasia bathed the women, first Charise and then Latisha, and hurriedly brought them clean clothes. She nearly dropped Latisha's dress when Andrew walked through the bathing room in his underwear, looking for hot water to rinse off with. Latisha, covered with a towel, smiled as she saw the look of fascination on Anastasia's face as she watched Andrew move about.

In the dining room of the inn, the family drank cold water and ate fresh fruit. Charise and Andrew waited for Latisha to explain herself. Finally, she put down a fresh peach she had been eating and began her story.

◆◆◆◆

The Field of Valor

Chapter the Fourteenth

As her foster mother and brother sat across the table from her, Latisha ordered bread, fruit and water. Anastasia, having delivered the food, returned to the kitchen. As she left the dining area, a shimmering screen appeared to encompass the room.

"It insures privacy," Latisha explained as Charise and Andrew looked around at the screen.

"My eternal name is Seth," Latisha began. "I am a sorcerer, but, unlike the sorcerers of the northlands, I choose to live in normal life cycles. Garand is the eldest of the northland sorcerers, and I had lived more than a hundred lifetimes before he was born."

She could see Andrew doing the math in his head, so Latisha volunteered, "Yes, Andrew, that's about three thousand years.

"I choose to whom I am born, and where and when. I live sometimes as a man, sometimes as a woman. I have been born on every continent except Antarctica, in every color, shape, and size you can imagine. Sometimes I live a rich, full life, and sometimes I die from battle, or childbirth, or just unlucky accidents. I live lifetimes in the world of science, others in the world of dragons.

"In this life, I chose to be born to a young woman who made a bad choice with a descendant of mine. I knew she would abandon me, and arranged to have her do so at your church. I hoped you would rescue me, and you did. I wanted to be close to Andrew, because I knew he would be special and hoped he would turn out as he has.

"Even I did not anticipate that you would keep me and raise me as your own, and that I would become a sister to Andrew." Pausing, she reached across the table and laid her hand on Andrew's. "And I never imagined you would become the man you are. My greatest hopes have been wildly exceeded."

She smiled as Andrew looked at the table in embarrassment.

"I gave my birth mother a blessing when she left me at the church, and she abandoned her reckless life in favor of education and a productive life and family. I made sure she never suffered from the guilt that is so common with women who make the choice she made-- while it was voluntary on her part, it was predictable and it served my needs well."

Latisha waited a few moments while Charise and Andrew processed what she had told them.

"You have seen me as Ayala," she said, mostly to Andrew. He looked thoughtful at first, and then smiled with recognition.

"Did you arrange for Angus to come live with us?" Charise asked.

"Nothing is coincidence," Latisha replied. "You know about Garth. He was my favorite dragon, but he went to face Angus knowing he would not prevail. I can see the possibilities of the future, and I knew Angus would slay Garth. It broke my heart for Garth to go, but he went willingly. We knew that Angus would be the key to saving the northlands from a very bleak future under the warlords of the East."

"Just what is your plan, then?" Andrew interrupted.

Latisha smiled.

"From this point on, I have none," she admitted frankly. "I know, in my heart, that Andrew will somehow play a key role in the days to come. I know Angus will be there, and that he has prepared Andrew well for whatever challenges lie ahead. But there are too many possibilities for me to predict the outcome with any accuracy.

"I only know that I am very troubled by the future, but I am hopeful that it will be a better future because of Andrew."

Andrew shook his head. "I don't know what you expect of me," he said, more harshly than he intended. "I'm not a soldier, a politician, or a sorcerer. I can't imagine what I can do to help these people when thousands of soldiers invade from the East."

"I don't know, either," Latisha admitted. "Just do what is right in your heart, and I believe it will turn out well."

The three sat silently for nearly an hour, each nibbling on bread and fruit and lost in their own thoughts. Charise and Andrew looked up suddenly as the shimmering privacy screen disappeared.

Ian walked into the room, covered with blood.

"The other raiding party has been destroyed," he announced emotionlessly.

"Do we have any casualties?" Latisha asked.

"No," Ian replied. "I found twenty dragonslayers, and with Erin's help we surprised them before they could make their raid on the village. As with the group here, there were about a hundred of them, and twenty dragonslayers made quick work of them."

Ian thought for a moment.

"Twenty dragonslayers and one dragon, that is. Erin found them, and she kept them from escaping once the battle had begun."

Latisha smiled. Ian, who had been emotionless, smiled back.

Charise watch the young couple and felt a quick tug of happiness in her heart. She knew those looks, and they told her more than any explanation ever would. Her foster daughter was a young woman in love, and the man she loved was equally smitten with her. She felt joy at the recognition of young love.

Then she remembered why they were here and felt sad again.

Suddenly, Garand appeared at the front door of the inn. Looking around, he saw the foursome at the table. He could not hide the surprise as he realized Ian was covered in blood.

Moving quickly across the inn to their table, he asked Ian, "What happened to you?"

"Raiding parties," Ian replied, "from the East. One here, one to our east. Both about a hundred men."

Garand was visibly shaken.

"Is everyone OK?" he asked.

"Yes," Ian replied. "There are funeral pyres burning right now for each of the raiding parties."

"You must tell me what happened," Garand demanded.

"Not now," Charise said, interrupting Ian. "What did you find out about the armies of the East?" she asked the old sorcerer.

"They are collecting on the east side of the mountains. It appears they will be coming through a pass just south of the dragon breeding grounds."

He looked concerned.

"There are hundreds of thousands of soldiers, some mounted on horses and some infantry. And there are dragons," he finished ominously.

"Are they ready to attack?" Ian asked.

"Not yet," Garand replied. "They are massing right now. There are a number of warlords involved, so they will have to work out their battle plans before they move. But they will have to move soon, or the winter will cut them off until springtime."

"More immediately," Garand interjected, "there is a great gathering at the meadow of the sword, as people have taken to calling it." Looking at Andrew, he added, "They are all there to see you meet your first dragon. It seems that news of your arrival has spread quickly, and your debut will be widely attended."

Charise watched Garand's face as he made the final announcement. She did not trust him fully, and she felt anger at the way in which Garand seemed to relish Andrew's first confrontation with a dragon. She almost suspected the old man was hoping the dragon would prevail.

Charise stood quickly, cutting off further conversation.

"I guess we'll be leaving in the morning, then," she said. "How long will it take to get to the "field of valor", as Angus calls it?" she asked, looking at Garand.

"Time means nothing here," he reminded her, "but you would expect to spend one night encamped on your way there."

"Fine," she said. "Then let's all get to bed and be ready to ride at first light."

"But I want to know about the raiding parties," Garand objected.

"There will be a long ride tomorrow, during which we will gladly share what we know of them. But, for now, we are all tired and need to rest."

It was her "mother" voice, and even Garand acquiesced to Charise's plan.

As Charise went into her room, she felt Latisha's hand on her arm.

"I'm sorry I deceived you," Latisha said quietly. "This is the first time I have had to announce my lineage to a mother, and I'm afraid circumstances made it more shocking than it should have been."

Charise smiled. "You've been a wonderful daughter," she said kindly. "I always knew you were special. I just didn't know how special until tonight.

"It's odd," she said quietly. "You are so ancient, and yet you are still a young girl in so many ways."

Latisha looked puzzled. "What makes you say that?" she asked.

"I see the way you and Ian look at each other," Charise said quietly, "and it's a look only a young girl and young man exchange."

Latisha laughed.

"Yes, I am quite fond of Ian," she whispered, "but if he had been born in the world of science, he would have listened to news of the American civil war with great interest."

Charise's surprise was obvious.

"Dragonslayers don't age like people in your world," Latisha explained, "or even like people in this world."

Charise looked thoughtful, then leaned over and kissed Latisha on the cheek.

"Good night," she said quietly. "I love you."

"Good night," Latisha responded. "And I love you, too."

Morning came quickly. Charise was downstairs before sunrise, awakening the innkeeper and getting him to send boys for the horses. Anastasia was still wiping sleep from her eyes as she rushed to prepare breakfast for the departing guests.

As the rest of the party came down the stairs, breakfast was waiting for them. The horses had been saddled, and the supplies were being loaded on the pack horse.

As they finished breakfast, Garand asked again about the raiding parties.

"Let's get on the road," Charise insisted. "There will be plenty of time during the trip to tell you all about it."

As they rode southeast, Charise began the story with the walk she and Latisha had taken. She did not mention the sword Latisha gave her, or the electric charge she had felt when she had taken it in her hand the first time. She hoped the old sorcerer would not ask how two previously unarmed women would come into the possession of swords and knowledge in how to use them.

Garand was not going to let such details pass.

"Do I understand that you fought off the soldiers until Erin and her mother arrived?" he asked Charise.

"Well," she replied, "Latisha was there to help. And Erin came almost immediately, as did Ian and Andrew."

"I'm surprised you even had a sword," Garand commented, "let alone knowing how to use one."

Charise smiled as sweetly as possible.

"We've lived with Angus for nearly a decade," she asserted. "Why would you be surprised that we had swords and knew how to use them?"

The old sorcerer looked doubtfully at her, but knew it was a waste of time to challenge her story. "Continue," he invited, looking at Ian. "This is important information."

It took most of the day to finish the tales of the raiding parties. Ian had a mind for detail, and the old sorcerer had what Charise thought were a million questions. She halted the tale during lunch, and Ian paused as they ferried across the channel, but the story was otherwise uninterrupted through the day.

At dusk, they stopped for the night in a secluded glade. Ian and Andrew cared for the horses while Charise and Latisha started the fire and prepared food.

Garand did not dismount when they stopped.

"I need to get to our destination," he explained, "to meet with the other sorcerers and share this news."

Charise was glad to see him go, and felt that the others were equally glad.

As the evening chill cut through her blankets, Charise missed Angus and his body warmth. She could see Ian and Latisha cuddled up together, and Andrew was already sound asleep.

At daybreak, Charise felt the warmth of the fire before she opened her eyes. Erin had arrived and had placed two logs on the fire pit. They were burning brightly, and Latisha was petting Erin, thanking her for the fire.

After a cold breakfast, the horses were again saddled and the party moved out. Erin was flying above them, watching for any danger and leading them directly to the meadow of the sword. Charise wondered if Angus had made it to the meadow yet, and how long it would be before she saw him.

As they topped a hill, Ian pointed to the mass of people gathered ahead.

"That's the meadow," he said. "I have never seen this many people gathered, though."

Charise scanned the mass of humanity, encamped in a semi-circle on the near side of the meadow.

"Why are they all on this side?" she asked Ian.

"Dragons are on the other side," he replied. "They are hard to see from here," he explained, "because they blend into the wood line behind them. But they are there, by the hundreds."

Charise rode in silence, trying not to think of Andrew facing a dragon. Suddenly, she couldn't hold her questions any longer.

"When will Andrew face his dragon?" she asked Ian.

"Probably this afternoon," Ian replied. "He will, without question, be first up in a field of many. I believe there are new dragonslayers here today, as well as those of us who are already in green armor."

"How many dragons, and how many dragonslayers, will there be?" she asked.

"A hundred or so of each," he replied.

"Who will pick the dragon Andrew has to face?"

"The dragons," Ian replied. "Considering his armor, it will be a green scale. I'm not sure how dragons pick their champions, but I'm sure he will have a good fight on his hands."

Ian had no idea how his final comment stabbed Charise's heart with fear.

The group rode in silence the rest of the way. Ian was visibly excited by the upcoming challenges, while Andrew scanned the crowd and seemed lost in his own thoughts. Latisha looked frequently at Charise, feeling her mother's fear.

The crowd parted as the company rode into the gathering. Erin landed on the human side of the meadow, and Ian instinctively rode toward her.

Angus and his novices were waiting when they arrived. As soon as the newcomers joined Angus, Erin changed her appearance to that of the beagle, standing beside Angus as if she were a loyal dog.

"Ian," Angus greeted the younger dragonslayer, who was first to arrive.

"Elder," Ian replied reverently.

"Andrew," Angus called out. "And ladies," he added, looking first at Charise, the Latisha, then back to Charise.

When the horses stopped, Angus walked directly to Charise. Reaching up, he helped her off her mount. The two stood there,

Angus' hands on Charise's waist. Everyone waited patiently until they finally parted, and Angus moved to shake hands with Andrew and Ian.

The novices and squires ran to help unsaddle and groom the horses. Angus walked to a circle of logs placed on the ground like benches. Andrew, Ian, Charise, and Latisha joined him as he sat.

Looking to Andrew, Angus asked, "Are you ready, lad?"

Charise was shocked.

"Already?" she asked. "We just arrived."

"Aye," Angus replied sympathetically. "But it's a long day with a large field of combatants. And they can't start until Andrew has had his time."

Charise did her best not to cry, but tears ran down her cheeks against her will. Andrew moved over to hold his mother.

"I'll be fine," he assured her.

Charise placed a lingering kiss on his cheek, then stood and straightened the front of her dress.

"Well," she said. "Tears won't help you, and they won't change anything. I guess it's time we got on with it."

Angus wanted to hold her, but he knew this was not the time.

Andrew walked to Angus. Pointing to a group of men, Angus directed, "Where the sorcerers gather will be the starting place. Let's go."

Charise watched as the only men in the world that mattered to her walked away.

◆◆◆◆

Facing the Dragon Fire

Chapter the Fifteenth

s they walked away from the group, Andrew suddenly stopped and turned to Angus.

"Can I have just a couple more minutes?" he asked the old dragonslayer.

"Aye," Angus replied, tentatively, "but just a few."

Andrew walked quickly back to Latisha.

The two spoke quietly for several minutes. Angus could see Latisha nodding as they spoke, agreeing with whatever Andrew was asking her. At one point, she laughed and shook her head, but the rest of the conversation was very serious. Finally, Andrew hugged his sister and walked resolutely back to Angus.

"Ready now?" Angus asked.

"Ready," Andrew replied.

The two men walked to where the sorcerers had gathered. Behind them, Latisha whispered to her mother, and then followed well behind the men.

Angus introduced Andrew to each of the seven sorcerers. Each sorcerer represented a different region, or province, of the western world. Garand was clearly the most senior among them, and he did most of the talking. Wishing Andrew luck, he pointed to the high stage constructed just behind where they were standing.

"Under the circumstances," Garand explained, "we thought you might want to address the crowd before you face the dragon."

Angus looked curiously at the old sorcerer, but kept his peace.

Andrew smiled. "Thank you. I would like that," he said, and walked to the stage.

Andrew's confidence grew with each step he took. The crowd roared when he reached the top and waived.

"Friends," he said, facing the crowd. His voice carried across the multitude as he spoke, and he could see that even the furthest groups could hear him.

Turning to the field, he drew his sword and placed its tip on the stage. Bowing over the sword, he said quietly, "Noble dragons."

The dragons lowered their heads in acknowledgement of his greeting.

Turning as he spoke, Andrew looked across the crowd and then the dragons.

"I came here today to face my first dragon," he began. "And that is what I will do. But I have come with a heavy heart, for this is a battle that always results in death. Sometimes it is a dragon, sometimes a man. But, either way, mothers cry and fathers grieve, whether those parents are dragon or man. It seems that we are willing to waste our finest men and most noble dragons in a contest that represents an ancient conflict. Somehow, it seems there should be a better way."

The crowd stood silently. Andrew waited, letting his words sink in.

"When I trained," he began again, "my master, the great Angus the Elder, used magic to shield me from injury, and to protect others from the strike of my sword. I believe that magic is the boon needed to make this a joyous contest instead of the bloodbath we have all come to expect."

Andrew made a full turn, trying to look at each member of the crowd and each dragon assembled across the glade.

"I propose," he said finally, "that Angus use that magic to protect me and the dragon I face from the fatal blow of the sword or consumption by the fire."

A murmur passed through the crowd. Andrew watched as they spoke among themselves, waiting for the right moment to finish.

"As in my world," he added, "the battle will proceed as usual. But, in the end, either the dragon will succeed in bathing me in fire, or I will make a final stroke to its neck. When that happens, Angus will declare the winner and the battle will be complete.

"By using this magic, we will have a decisive contest without destroying either man or dragon. And, I am assured by a great sorcerer, the magic and courage which passes in the fatal contest will be equally strong without the loss of life."

Garand was moving toward the stage when the crowd roared its approval. Looking around, he returned to his place among the sorcerers.

Andrew turned to the dragons.

"Who have you chosen as champion?" he asked.

A giant green scale stepped forward.

"My name is Andrew. May I know your name, noble dragon?" he asked.

"Valborga," came the reply.

Andrew dismounted the stage and walked within a few feet of the dragon. Drawing his sword, he knelt and bowed his head.

Valborga knelt and bowed.

Andrew stood, as did Valborga.

Angus walked up behind Andrew. Andrew turned as Angus touched his shoulder, feeling the familiar shock pass through him and his sword.

Angus looked past Andrew at the great green scale. Briefly bowing his head, he smiled and said to Valborga, "It is good to see you again, old friend."

The dragon smiled. "It is an honor to again be in the presence of Angus, Slayer of Garth. 'Tis a different meadow, and I am now well rested."

Angus nodded. "Are the new rules acceptable to the dragons?"

Valborga nodded. "I have lost three children to this field," she replied. "If this magic can help my young survive as they learn, it is, indeed, a boon." Motioning over her shoulder at the other dragons, she finished, "The others feel the same as I."

Angus bowed his head briefly. Turning, he returned to the edge of the meadow, standing next to Latisha and Charise.

Andrew raised his sword to the ready, holding it in front of him.

Valborga turned and launched into the air in a single movement.

The fight was joined.

Hour after hour, the battle continued between Valborga and Andrew. Each time the great green moved in and blew fire at Andrew, the young man moved deftly aside. Each strike of Andrew's sword found only air, because Valborga moved quickly out of range.

As the sun set, Valborga landed in front of Andrew. Bowing her head, she said, "This day is done, and the battle is not yet settled. We will begin again in the morn."

Andrew placed the tip of his sword in the ground and bowed his head.

"You are a noble adversary," he said quietly. "I look forward to continuing."

With a mighty flap of her wings, the dragon took flight. Andrew sheathed his sword and turned toward his teacher, mother and sister.

The crowd roared with approval.

As he reached his family, Andrew whispered to Angus, "I don't know if I could have gone on. I am SO tired!"

Angus smiled. "Aye, Lad. It was a magnificent fight. And tomorrow you will continue. You need food, and rest."

Within an hour, Andrew had eaten and was sleeping soundly. The crowd still milled about. Food and drink vendors were moving through the crowds. Everyone in the crowd was still talking about the day's battle, and reliving the moves of both the dragon and Andrew.

Charise sat next to Angus, nibbling on some melon he had procured as dessert.

"Why is it taking so long?" she asked the old dragonslayer.

"They are both great fighters," Angus replied. "I have been to this meadow thousands of times, and only once have I seen a dragon with such skill. Valborga was well chosen to face our Andrew.

"And Andrew is equal to the skill of even this dragon. He moves well, staying just out of the reach of the fire. I have never had a student who could fight this well."

Charise sat quietly for a moment before asking, "Are you sure the magic will protect them when the end comes?"

"I am," Latisha said from behind them.

Angus and Charise turned, surprised to see Latisha and Ian standing behind them.

Charise was relieved, but both Angus and Ian looked unsure. "How can you be so sure?" asked Ian.

Latisha smiled. "I know this magic, and I am sure it is sufficient to protect them both." Leaning over to kiss Ian, she said, "Let's find a place to be alone."

Ian smiled, taking her hand as they walked away through the crowd.

"She is Ayala, and Ayala is Seth," Angus observed absently. "Is there anything else I should know about her?"

Charise looked at him in wonder. "How did you know that?" she asked.

"I don't know," he replied. "Someone made Andrew's voice carry to the crowd, and let the dragons understand him as well. The only explanation that made any sense was that it was her."

Charise kissed the old dragonslayer on the cheek.

"You are amazing," she observed affectionately.

Angus smiled.

As the sun came up, the crowd began to shift. Everyone was trying to find a vantage point where they could see as much of the meadow as possible. As the family ate a silent breakfast, Andrew finally asked Angus, "Any advice for today?"

"Just keep your wits about you," Angus replied quietly, "and don't forget to dodge the fire."

Andrew laughed.

Valborga returned to the meadow as the dew was burning off under the morning sun. Having received the magic touch from Angus, Andrew returned to his station.

Dragon and dragonslayer bowed, and the giant green dragon took to the sky.

The morning battle was as breathtaking as the previous afternoon. Again and again, Andrew seemed to make impossible moves to escape the fire. Again and again, the dragon twisted just out of reach of Andrew's sword.

As the sun reached the noonday peak, Valborga came at Andrew, pausing for just a second at the end of her approach in an attempt to throw the dragonslayer's timing off.

Andrew ran three steps and struck the dragon on his neck with the sword.

The crowd went wild. Dragons screeched and pounded their tales.

Andrew and Valborga faced each other.

Valborga bowed her head, acknowledging defeat.

Andrew sheathed his sword and, facing Valborga, bowed from the waist.

Turning to the crowd, Andrew bowed again. The roar became nearly deafening, and only decreased when he stood upright.

Stepping to his right, Andrew looked to the dragons gathered on the far end of the meadow. Slowly, he bowed. The dragons responded with screeching and tail pounding which shook the ground under Andrew's feet.

As the roar died down, Andrew walked right up to Valborga's face. Mimicking the movements he had watched his sister use with Erin, he placed his left hand under the giant green chin and scratched the flat spot on the top of the dragon's head.

Valborga's eyes closed; the pleasure was clear on her face.

"Noble Valborga," Andrew said softly. "You are a queen among dragons. I will forever be your friend and comrade. If you should ever need my services, please ask. My life and my blade are forever at your service."

Valborga's eyes opened. Andrew felt her head nod.

Turning away from the dragon, Andrew returned to his family on the sidelines.

Again, the crowd went wild.

As Andrew reached his mother, Charise grabbed him and hugged him so tight and so long he was actually losing his breath. Latisha hugged him and kissed his cheek. Ian shook his hand vigorously.

Andrew looked to Angus. The old dragonslayer reached out and tapped him on his chest plate.

Looking down, Andrew realized his armor now had a luminescent turquoise glow, just like Angus'. Looking quickly across the meadow, he saw that Valborga's scales had the same color and glow.

Angus smiled at the lad. Without a word, he turned and walked to the next contestant.

By the end of the day, six more battles had been fought. Four dragons and two young dragonslayers would have met their fate that day, but because of Angus' magic they would all live to fight another day. The crowd loved the action, even knowing no one would die on the field.

All in all, Andrew thought as the day ended, it's been a pretty good day. He was standing next to Angus, who was having a pleasant chat with a grandmotherly woman who couldn't seem to stop touching him.

Suddenly, three young women ran up to Andrew and grabbed him by the arms. Before he realized what was happening, they were pulling him away.

Andrew looked to Angus, who simply smiled and nodded, as did the old woman he was talking to. Andrew let the girls lead him away, and Angus returned to his conversation.

Not far away, Charise and Latisha were watching as the girls led Andrew into the crowd.

"I hope they're not going where I think they're going," Charise commented absently.

"Oh, yes, they are!" laughed Latisha.

Charise fell quiet for a moment, still watching Angus and the woman.

"Are you OK?" Latisha asked.

"Yes," Charise said lightly. "I was just watching that woman with Angus. They must have known each other for a long time."

Latisha smiled, shaking her head. "She 'knew' Angus when she was just a maiden," she said knowingly.

Charise turned to Latisha. Although the question was unspoken, Latisha understood what Charise wanted to know.

"Yes, she 'knew' him in the biblical sense," Latisha teased. "As had her mother, her grandmother, and now her daughter."

The shock was apparent on Charise's face.

"It's a cultural thing," Latisha explained. "Look around you. Except the dragonslayers, everyone you see is a farmer or merchant. They work sunup to sundown, and the work is hard--remember, there are no tractors here, no delivery trucks.

"Women grow up on farms and marry farmers. Others grow up in stores and marry merchants. They have children, raise them, and die. That's the cycle of life in this world. Little education, no movies or dances. Just husbands and kids.

"It's not surprising that the young girls want to have a fling with a dragonslayer before they settle down and start a family. They know there's no chance of marriage, no hope of children, but they have one or two nights of pleasure and make memories for a lifetime.

"That old lady over there spends many evenings in her rocker, smiling at the memory of a night long ago when she was a maid and seduced a dragonslayer. And, after all these years, she still wants to see him, touch him, speak to him...he's a part of her life she'll treasure forever."

Charise tipped her head slightly in thought. Latisha watched her, waiting for her response. Charise said nothing, but a small smile crept onto her face. She was facing in Angus' direction, but her gaze went off into nowhere.

"Mom!" Latisha urged. Charise looked at her, still smiling.

"Are you jealous?" Latisha asked.

Charise laughed silently. "No, of course not!"

Latisha looked at her mother carefully. Charise looked away, somehow nervous about what her daughter might see.

"Mom, you remember what you said about being in love with a white guy a hundred years older than you?"

"Yes," Charise replied.

"I don't think so," Latisha observed.

"Why not?" Charise asked.

"Because, if you were, you would have taken that old woman's head off by now!" Latisha laughed.

"But I really do care about him," Charise observed quietly. "I miss him when he's gone. I rely on him." Pausing, she added, "If I'm not in love, then what is this?"

Latisha smiled. "Friends," she said simply. "Very good friends, caught up in something that has kept you close for a long time. But I don't think you are romantically involved, or you wouldn't think it was 'cute' that Angus has known all these women."

Charise kissed her daughter on the cheek. "I'll have to think about that," she said quietly. Looking around, she asked, "Where's that young man of yours?"

Latisha smiled. "He's waiting for me," she said in a conspiratorial tone. "I'm not worried--he knows better than to let these girls distract him."

Charise laughed.

"Then, go!" she said. "I'll worry over my relationship with Angus without any more help from you."

Latisha kissed her mother, and then disappeared into the crowd.

Charise walked over to Angus, who was finishing his conversation with the older lady. Charise recognized the look the old woman gave her as she took Angus' arm; it was envy.

"Old friend?" she asked Angus casually.

"Aye," he responded. "I knew her many summers ago. She is here with her family. Her son was one of the successful dragonslayers this afternoon."

Charise smiled, and then kissed him on the cheek.

"Are you going to the party?" she asked him. "There seems to be plenty of young girls to go around."

Angus smiled. "Not tonight," he said. "I prefer your company, as long as you will bless me with it."

Charise hugged the old dragonslayer, kissing him again.

"I don't know what to think of you," she laughed. "But being with you makes me happy, so stick around as long as you want."

Angus smiled and nodded. "Dinner?" he asked.

When Charise nodded, he took her hand and led her away to a vendor selling baked chicken.

••••

Prince Andrew

Chapter the Sixteenth

It took four days to complete the contests. All of Angus' young dragonslayers were successful; others did not fare so well. The true impact of the change in fighting rules came at the end, when no funeral pyres burned for the dragons, and no hearses carried away the charred remains of young men.

Instead, there was joy all around. And tales to be told for years to come, without the pain of loss that normally followed these contests.

Of all the ideas Andrew would ever have, Angus believed this was probably the best.

The most surprising side-effect of the change began on day two. Erin had been spending some time with the dragons, and some time with Angus. When she was among the dragons, she was in her dragon form. When she was among the people, she shifted to her dog persona.

Day two, mid-day, Valborga landed just at the edge of the meadow, next to where Andrew watched the contests with his mother and sister. As she landed, she changed into a Neapolitan Mastiff. Shortly afterwards, the dragon who had faced Ian earlier in the day arrived, turning into a Jack Russell terrier as he landed.

One by one, the dragons that had been defeated by dragonslayers arrived, changing into dogs of all varieties. Angus quickly realized what the dragons had discovered; a twenty or thirty foot dragon was too big to be among a crowd of people, but a dog fit in well. As each dragonslayer succeeded, they were making the same speech to the vanquished dragon that Andrew had made to Valborga. The dragons were responding by joining the dragonslayers, using the transformation in the same way Erin used it--to fit in among people.

As a rule, the dragons that had prevailed chose not to join their opponent after the contest.

As the crowd dispersed, the dragonslayers gathered around Andrew at the edge of the meadow, many accompanied by their dragons in the form of dogs. Charise stood a short distance away, accompanied by Angus and Latisha.

"Aren't you going to join them?" Charise asked Angus.

"No," Angus answered quietly. "It's Andrew's time. I would be a distraction."

Charise looked at the old dragonslayer and could see the pride in his face as he watched the dragonslayers take turns speaking with Andrew.

"I need you to come with me," Latisha said, taking Angus by the arm.

"I'll wait here," Charise volunteered.

"That would be good," Latisha agreed, kissing her mother on the cheek.

Charise watched Latisha and Angus walk toward the sorcerers, who were still gathered by the stage. As Latisha and Angus arrived, all of the sorcerers moved away from Garand and stood next to the newcomers.

Garand stood fast, watching the others move away. As he fully realized what was happening, his face showed his concern.

"So you are Seth," he said to Latisha.

"Yes," she confirmed.

"I should have known," Garand said quietly.

"There was a great effort to keep it from you," Latisha explained. "We knew of your visits to the East, and it was important to deceive you until the time was right."

"How did you know?" Garand asked.

"We are sorcerers," Latisha answered in a matter-of-fact voice. "It is difficult to keep your movements secret, especially when you take magic to places where it does not dwell naturally."

"So, what happens now? Am I to be destroyed, or exiled?"

"Neither is necessary," Latisha responded, "unless you force us to make such a choice."

Garand looked confused. "What, then?" he asked.

"The battle that is forming is a battle among men. And dragons. Our involvement will only make the outcome more destructive.

"We," she added, motioning to the other sorcerers, "know that you have worked throughout your life to maintain this world as it was when you first fully developed your powers. You have chosen to use your magic to preserve yourself, and the others were trained by you to do the same. Your intentions were honorable--you wanted to avoid the wars and destruction you saw in the world of science by preventing the development of kingdoms with standing armies. You believed, rightfully, that the rulers would use those armies to maintain and expand their own power, just as it has happened again and again in the world of science.

"What you did not understand is that every choice has a price," Latisha explained. "While you kept the northlands from organizing beyond villages, others were building armies and inevitably saw the possibility of raiding these provinces. I was able to prevent that in the first dragon war by providing you with my dragons. The warlords of the East have advanced in their tactics and numbers, so I can no longer protect these provinces.

"It is time for these lands to progress," she concluded. "They must develop the means to protect themselves, and that means creating governments and raising armies. For now, they are dependent upon the dragonslayers and dragons, and we hope that will be enough.

"As for you," she finished, "we hold no ill will. You have spent your life preserving yourself, and you shifted allegiances because you saw the way of life here as doomed." Pausing, she looked away before returning her attention to Garand. "You have done much good, though, and it would be wrong to forget that because of a lapse in judgment. As long as you do not become further involved in this conflict, there is no reason you should be banished or destroyed."

Garand was confused but relieved. After a long pause, he looked along the line of sorcerers and replied, "I understand. I will remain neutral, and we will see what happens."

Latisha smiled.

"But," Garand asked, "what if they find the Orb of Solomon? Will we still remain neutral if they gain the advantage of the Orb?"

The sorcerers looked to Latisha. Slowly, she raised her right arm, palm down. As her arm reached full extension and was parallel to the ground, a glow came from her palm. When the glow had resolved itself into a ball of intense light, Latisha turned her palm up and held the newly formed orb.

"This," she said quietly, "is what many have known as the Orb of Solomon."

The sorcerers stared silently at the small globe.

"However," she added, "they misunderstand the nature of the Orb. The orb is not this little light--it was simply a way to focus attention on the powers it represents. I," she paused for emphasis, "am the Orb. I lay with Solomon every night, replenishing his energy and granting him access to magic. It was my energy and counsel that helped him rule, and which established the Hebrew nation in the land of science.

"There is no chance the warlords of the east will gain access to the Orb," she concluded, "since I am standing here with you."

Each sorcerer watched as the globe disappeared. Latisha watched silently as they spoke among themselves, and Garand stepped forward to join the others. The circle of sorcerers was again complete, but Garand was no longer first among peers. As they began to confer among themselves, Latisha announced, "Let us remain here as the battle is joined," she announced. Each sorcerer agreed, in turn, including Garand. "There will be much for us to do, depending on the outcome of the battle."

Angus turned to leave. Latisha turned to him and asked, "Will you be joining the dragonslayers?" she asked.

"I will do as Andrew wishes," he responded.

Latisha smiled and nodded. Angus walked toward the assembled dragonslayers.

Each dragonslayer had approached Andrew in turn, and he had shared what he knew of the gathering armies to the east. As Angus approached, they all turned to the old dragonslayer. Angus walked up to Andrew and put his hand on his shoulder.

"Well, Lad," he said in a voice that all could hear, "it seems you are a Prince in a land with no kingdoms. What would you have us do?"

Andrew sighed. "I may be a prince," he replied, "but I have no right to lead unless that is the choice of the people."

Without hesitation, everyone drew their swords and held them high in the air, indicating their loyalty to Andrew.

"Then we need to prepare. The armies of the East are huge," he began. "We will need to use our heads as well as our swords to defeat them."

A murmur went through the crowd indicating their agreement.

"Dragonslayers will be the only hope of success," Andrew continued. "But we need more than just swords. Armies are not just soldiers--they need food and transportation. Do you believe the people from your villages will be willing to give us the food and help we need?"

Andrew paused as the dragonslayers discussed his question. As consensus developed, they agreed that they could count on the villagers to support their efforts with food and transportation.

"There are many who trained as dragonslayers," Angus suggested, "who chose a different path. They are trained with swords and knives, and may be willing to join our ranks."

A murmur of agreement passed through the crowd. Every man present began to consider old classmates that had chosen family and village over the life of a dragonslayer.

"Go, then," Andrew instructed. "Find your classmates and tell them of the danger. Go to the farms and ask for them to provide livestock and vegetables for the Army. We will need butchers and millers, cooks and bakers. All of that must be transported to our camp, and we will need blacksmiths with steel to prepare weapons for those who have none, and to repair the wagons and weapons.

"Take only what they can spare, and recruit only the willing," Andrew added. "We serve the people. When you have a sword and they don't, it's easy to start seeing it the other way around."

A murmur of agreement passed through the ranks.

"We will gather at the pass south of the dragon breeding grounds," he finished. "I will go there now, to scout the pass and develop a plan to defend it with the resources we have."

The dragonslayers dispersed quickly. Andrew turned to Angus and asked, "Will you go with me to the pass?"

Angus smiled. "Aye," he agreed. Looking down at Erin, he asked, "Will you be joining us?"

Erin moved closer to Angus' leg to show her agreement.

Andrew felt pressure on his leg. Looking down, he realized Valborga was indicating that she would stay with him.

Angus smiled. "It appears we will be traveling with dragons," he observed.

"Thank God!" Andrew responded.

The two men walked to Charise, who had been preparing a simple dinner, waiting for everyone to finish their business. Latisha left the sorcerers and joined them.

Andrew, Angus, and Latisha shared the new developments with Charise over dinner. She was unhappy with the decision about Garand, and felt he was still a threat.

"Mom," Latisha said seriously, "one of the oldest rules of combat is to keep your friends close, your enemies closer." Pausing, she added, "Garand will either join the sorcerers and be an asset, or he will try to return to the East, in which case we will know where he is. Either way," she concluded, "there is no sense in worrying. He holds his fate in his own hands. Now it is up to him."

Charise's face still showed disagreement, but she let it pass for the moment.

"Will you be staying here with the other sorcerers?" she asked.

"Yes."

"Then keep an eye on him. Please?" Charise asked.

"Of course," Latisha reassured her.

Turning to the men, Charise asked, "When do we leave for the mountains?"

Andrew spoke first. "It's going to be very dangerous, Mom," he pleaded, "so it would be better if you stayed at the Inn until we returned."

Charise smiled at her son. Reaching into the front of her dress, she drew the sword Latisha had given her and held it upright in front of her face. Light from the campfire reflected off its surface as she said quietly, "If it's going to be dangerous, I will keep this close at hand. But I will NOT be staying behind."

Andrew started to say something, but felt Angus' hand on his arm. A glance at the old dragonslayer confirmed what he already knew; there was no point in arguing with his mother.

After dinner, the talk turned to the events of the past four days. Ian had gone to his home village, so Latisha remained with her family. Everyone took the time to congratulate Andrew on his idea to use magic to stop the bloodshed; there was no mention of his battle with Valborga, who was lying next to him in her dog form.

As the conversation died out, Valborga and Erin moved among the family, getting scraps of food and strokes from each member in turn. Charise was scratching Valborga behind the ears, wishing she had a dragon, when Erin's mother landed just outside the camp.

As she landed, the dragon morphed into an English Bulldog. She walked directly to Charise, standing in front of her with her head in Charise's lap. Charise petted her head, and the dog/dragon's tail wagged appreciatively.

"It appears you have been adopted by a dragon," Angus mused.

Charise took the dog's head in her hand and looked directly into her eyes. "Do you want to stay with me?" she asked.

The dog's excitement was obvious.

"What is your name?" Charise asked.

The dog barked, but Charise did not understand.

"Addiena," Angus translated. "It means 'beautiful.'"

Latisha reached out and touched her mother on the shoulder. "You will need to understand your dragon," she said. Charise felt the energy pass through her body. "They don't say much, but when they talk it is usually for a reason."

Andrew was first to unroll his blanket and lie down, Valborga lying at his feet. Erin and Addiena played for a few minutes more, then settled down next to Angus and Charise. Latisha spread out her blanket next to Andrew.

Charise and Angus talked quietly for a while longer, and then spread their blankets out together. As they lay down, Erin and Addiena curled up together at their feet.

As dawn crept over the horizon, Charise awoke to a blazing campfire. Erin had again started a fire while her family slept. As each member of the family awoke, they moved to the fire to break the chill of the morning air.

Angus was cooking eggs, ham, and an orange vegetable that looked like sweet potatoes. The smell made Charise's stomach rumble.

"Can I help?" she asked.

"No, thank you," Angus replied affectionately. "Just get a plate and enjoy. This will be the last hot breakfast we will have for a while."

As Charise filled her plate, Erin, Valborga, and Addiena gathered around her.

Latisha moved next to her mother, wiping sleep from her eyes. Scratching Erin between her ears, she said, "Go find your own breakfast. There will not be enough here for three hungry dragons."

Erin and Addiena trotted out of the camp. As they reached the edge of the meadow, each dog transformed into a dragon and took to the sky. Valborga sat where she was.

"Go," Latisha said sweetly to the dog. "We will be fine until you get back."

Reluctantly, Valborga walked away. As she transformed and took flight, Andrew looked at his sister.

"What was that about?" he asked.

"She was going to stay here to protect us," Latisha responded. "Dragons are very protective of humans, once they have bonded."

"What do they eat?" Charise asked.

"Deer, elk, moose--sometimes a bear. Yellow scales eat a lot of fish, rabbits, and raccoons, but a full grown green scale needs about a hundred or more pounds per day, so smaller animals are not an efficient food source."

Charise smiled. "I'm glad they feed themselves," she observed, then took a bite of eggs with a small chunk of ham.

Latisha laughed, picking up a plate and filling it.

As they finished breakfast, Andrew and Angus gathered the blankets and folded them into the saddles of the pack horse. Charise and Latisha washed the breakfast dishes and passed them to the men to be loaded. Within the hour, the camp was packed and the fire was cold.

Angus, Andrew, and Charise each said their goodbyes to Latisha and mounted their horses.

"We will be in the village just south of here," Latisha told them. "If you need me, just call out my name and I will hear you."

The troop headed across the meadow and onto a trail that led east. Angus, who had traveled this trail many times, was in the lead. Charise rode second, and Andrew followed in the rear with the pack horse in tow. The trail was too narrow to ride abreast, so they rode in silence, each lost in their own thoughts.

High overhead, three giant green dragons flew in a loose formation.

An hour into the trip, they crossed an open meadow covered with flowers. The smell was wonderful, and Charise breathed deeply. For a moment, she forgot all about the battle to come and enjoyed the simple beauty of this strange world.

◆◆◆

Preparing for Battle

Chapter the Seventeenth

As Angus, Andrew and Charise drew close to the mountains; they stopped and spent the night in the forest. It was a cold camp, since they did not know where the Eastern armies might have spies.

As they sat silently after dinner, Andrew looked at Angus.

"Have you ever been in a battle with a large number of men?" he asked the Elder.

"No," Angus replied.

"I have no idea what is going to happen," Andrew said, sadly.

"Nor I," Angus agreed.

"Their troops will be battle-hardened," Charise volunteered. "Garand was at least honest about that. They have already conquered the lands to the East of the mountains."

It was several minutes before Andrew observed, "We can't let them get where they can spread out and get into formation. In my vision at Machu Picchu, I could see them moving this way up the eastern slopes, and they had to break formation to get around the rocks. They were also using the dragons to attack from above."

Angus and Charise looked at Andrew.

"I think we need to make our stand where the rocks are narrowest," Andrew said finally. "If my vision is correct, the dragons will have a problem with the updrafts, which may be what we need to do some damage."

"Aye, Lad," Angus agreed. "How are we going to fight men and dragons at the same time?"

"We'll have to have dragonslayers guarding the aerial attack, and others fighting the ground troops. I think we need to have them dedicated to one or the other; if they try to do both, it will be too easy to attack while we are distracted."

Angus nodded.

As night fell, everyone started getting ready for bed. As Andrew spread his blanket, he walked to where his mother was straightening the blanket for her and Angus.

"I think the dragons need to stay on the ground and keep their dog form," he said. His tone indicated clearly that he wanted his mother's agreement.

"Why?" she asked. "They are wonderful scouts."

"I don't want the spies to see them," Andrew responded. "If they know we have dragons, they will develop tactics to deal with them. If Garand told them that the dragons were not supporting us, as he told us when we first arrived, I want them to continue to believe that."

"It is a difficult choice," Angus volunteered, walking back from the horses. "Without the dragons in the sky, we will only know what we can see from the ground. But if they know we have dragons, we will not have the element of surprise."

Andrew looked at the old dragonslayer. "And?" he asked.

"And I will do as you wish," the Elder responded.

"Then we will ask them to remain in their dog forms," Andrew decided.

Angus nodded.

Charise stepped over and kissed her son. "Don't worry," she reassured him, "you're doing the right thing."

They had been sleeping for several hours when Valborga nuzzled Andrew and woke him. He sat up, sensing that his dragon was troubled. "Mom! Angus!"

Angus and Charise sat up.

"What's wrong, girl?" he asked the dragon.

The dog whined, but they all understood. She could feel her children calling her, and she wanted to go home to the breeding grounds.

"Go, Girl!" Andrew said, holding her head in his hands. "We'll be fine."

Erin and Addiena watched Valborga run to the west. The sky was overcast, so she disappeared almost immediately in the darkness of the night. After several minutes, Erin turned to Angus.

"She's taken wing," Angus reported.

They all sat up for a few minutes, then lay back down. Within minutes, they were asleep.

Erin and Addiena looked at each other as the deep breathing of sleep came from the three humans. Without a sound, they turned and disappeared silently into the night.

Angus awoke to Erin's cold nose. Before he was even fully awake, Angus was standing and had his hand on his sword.

Andrew was a split second behind Angus. His hand was also on his sword.

Charise looked up. Without hesitation she stood up and reached inside her dress for her sword.

Erin and Addiena turned and walked into the forest. Without breaking camp, the three followed on foot.

Half way up the ridge, the dogs stopped; they were hiding in place. Andrew looked around the edge of the rock--two soldiers were standing on the top of a boulder, looking out across the forest. They were pushing each other, playing around instead of searching. Andrew's last thought before ducking back behind the boulder was that the soldiers were standing in the open, with the sun shining behind them--not exactly the type of behavior he would expect from "battle hardened" troops.

Andrew spoke quietly to Angus and his mother, explaining what he had seen. Quickly, they discussed what to do.

"They don't know we're here," Angus observed. "We could just leave them be."

Andrew nodded.

"No," Charise said quietly.

Both men looked at her.

"No one who has come across the mountains to the West has returned. Two raiding parties came, and they all died. It seems to me we should make sure these two do not return. A consistent failure to return after crossing the ridge may give us a psychological advantage."

Angus and Andrew looked at each other; both nodded.

"But what do we do with the bodies?" Angus asked Charise.

Before they could discuss it more, Addiena and Erin trotted off. All three humans knew where they were headed and what they were going to do.

The two dogs trotted up behind the boulder where the men stood. Addiena barked, and then barked again.

The two men turned and looked over the East side of the boulder. As the soldiers smiled at the dogs, the canines morphed into dragons and each swallowed a man whole.

Two dogs returned to where Angus, Andrew, and Charise stood.

Andrew looked at Erin, asking silently if there were any more scouts. The dog shook her head.

Andrew led the way as the three made their way to the crest which overlooked the mountain pass.

About ten miles down the slopes, there was a plateau that stretched as far as Andrew could see in all directions. Soldiers were camped all over the plateau in what appeared to be five major camps. They were not in formation; they were in garrison. On the Eastern end of the plateau, Andrew could see wagons coming into camp, carrying supplies to the Armies.

In turn, Angus and Charise peeked over the crest.

After they had all had a look, Andrew climbed back up and looked again. Red dragons were gathering, away from the various garrisons and in a common area. Andrew climbed back down.

"I think they are going to attack with the dragons," he announced. "It looks like the dragons are being consolidated into a single group, instead of being with the garrisons."

Angus and Charise both nodded their agreement.

"Mom," Andrew said quietly, "I think I need you to go to the camp where the dragonslayers are gathering with the villagers and farm families."

Addiena moved close to Charise's leg.

"What do you want me to tell them?" she asked.

"Tell them we fear an attack by the dragons," he said. "Tell them we believe the dragons will be sent to kill those in the camp."

Charise nodded.

Angus looked down at Erin, tilting his head as if listening carefully to soft conversation. Nodding, he looked up.

"The dragons in the breeding grounds know," he said. "Those that choose to go to the camp will do so now."

"Ask them to take their animal forms," Andrew requested of Erin. "I do not want the red dragons to know they are here until the last moment."

Erin barked.

The family made their way back to camp. Erin and Addiena stayed behind, searching for other guards. They would insure that no one crossed over to the Western slopes.

As Charise mounted her horse and turned to the West, Addiena reappeared and stood to the right of Charse's horse.

Charise blew a kiss to the two men, then kicked her horse and headed west with Addiena following close behind.

Andrew and Angus began to clear camp silently. As they packed the horses, each man thought about how much he missed Charise. She had been gone less than an hour when they finished, but both felt like it had been a month.

"We need to hide the mounts," Angus said, breaking the silence.

"Let's head south," Andrew said. "The trees were thickest to the south and down the slopes."

Angus nodded and turned his horse down the hillside.

By late afternoon, they had found a pasture for the horses. Erin appeared as they released the horses.

Another pair of soldiers had crossed over to the West, looking for their comrades. Later, three soldiers crossed over, looking for them. Just before dark, five soldiers came looking for the others.

None would be returning to the East.

Angus showed Andrew how to make a pack out of his blanket. The two men headed back up the mountain, keeping the trees between them and the crest of the pass. As the moon rose high and the night became cooler, they made a quick camp inside a cave. Erin reappeared, lying at Angus' back and sharing his warmth.

At daybreak, Angus and Andrew were back on the path to the pass. Erin had already left before they awoke.

As they returned to the boulder where they had spied on the troops the day before, Erin reappeared.

The search parties were growing. The last one was ten soldiers. Erin was happily full; apparently, ten men is just the right number for a dragon's breakfast.

They moved around the crest until they found a boulder they could lie on their stomachs and watch the movements below. The cluster of dragons continued to grow, and the dragon handlers were sending them to fly, one by one. After a while, they began flying several at once--circling together, watching the handlers. When a handler held up a chicken, the dragon would attack in a dive and take it from the handler's grasp without landing. Angus watched with interest.

"They do not fight the way our dragons do," he observed. "They are smaller, faster, and do not land before attacking."

Pushing away from the ledge, Angus rolled over on his back. "We need to tell the people who have gathered. They will need to know."

Andrew thought for a moment. "Perhaps you should go tell them. Maybe you could use the trip to consider the best tactics."

Angus thought for a moment.

"Probably," he said thoughtfully. He was troubled by the idea of leaving Andrew here alone.

The two men continued to watch the camp as the day wore on. As the sun set, Erin returned to the boulder where they lay.

The search parties were growing. The last one was twenty. Erin noted that they moved very, very slowly. Their formations were more like clusters. They were afraid--very afraid.

Andrew and Angus were very happy to hear that news.

As they opened their minds to Erin, she quickly grasped the situation.

Erin barked, and then barked again.

Andrew and Angus both understood. Erin would fly back to the camp in the rear and pass the information on to the people and dragons gathered there. She could return before daybreak, and the army gathered to the East would not see her.

The biggest risk was that Angus and Andrew would be left without a dragon. Since the search parties were growing larger, the two men would have to deal with them. While there was no doubt that two dragonslayers could easily deal with 40 or 50 men, there was be a good chance that someone would escape and return to the garrisons. That would leave them vulnerable to a mass attack, and even Angus and Andrew would have a tough time if they massed several hundred men and attacked.

Erin left, running down the hill before transforming and launching into low level, high speed flight. Angus and Andrew climbed back up on their boulder, watching the garrisons below.

As the dew fell and the first glow of light came onto the eastern horizon, Angus and Andrew watched hundreds of red dragons take to the skies. Rolling off the boulder, the two men disappeared into the shadows.

As the dragons took to the sky, they circled over the garrisons, lining up in broad ranks as the new dragons entered the aerial formation. Each flight pattern was wider, and hundreds of dragons joined each time the leaders completed a circle.

When the dragon corrals were empty, the leaders headed West in lines that were a hundred dragons wide. By the time they were all airborne and formed up, the sun was glowing just below the eastern horizon.

The sky was red with dragons. Andrew felt his heart fall, watching them and knowing that his mother was among the people that they were targeting.

As the sky finally cleared, Erin ran up the hill and stood next to Angus. She had made it to the camp, and hundreds of dragons had joined the people who were gathered there. She also reported that the dragonslayers were almost all there, and their old classmates had joined them. There were now hundreds of people, and hundreds of dogs running at their feet. They were making preparations for the possible attack.

Erin had seen the red dragons in time to land and transform into a dog. None of the red dragons had paid any attention to her. Andrew could sense that she was almost disappointed; no matter how many red dragons there were, she was a great green scale and she wanted to show them what that really meant.

Angus patted her, assuring her there would be a time when she could show herself. After they had enjoyed a few moments together, she looked up and let them know she would be back on patrol for more soldiers. When Angus stood up from petting her, she turned and headed out. As she left, Andrew thought he heard her say something about all that flying making her hungry.

Andrew kept looking to the west, watching the trailing edge of the formation until it was out of sight.

Angus patted him on the back.

"No use watching them now, Lad," Angus observed sadly. "We need to focus on the ones that remain."

Slowly, the two men mounted their boulder and looked over the edge at the men in the camps below.

With most of the dragons gone, the garrisons were beginning to gather in more distinct patterns. There were still five identifiable groups, but they were lining up on each other to make a broad, deep formation. It was clear that they were going nowhere today, but it would not be long before they started to the west.

After mid-day, Erin returned, accompanied by Valborga. They reported that almost a hundred men had come forth in a search party. The soldiers had moved slowly, hiding behind boulders as they moved. It was clear that they did not want to go up the hill, and the officers were literally beating the soldiers to get them to move.

Erin and Valborga were preparing to strike when the men broke ranks and ran down the hill. The officers, left with a skeletal crew, headed back down the hill. The dragons let them leave, since they had not made it to the crest of the pass.

Clearly, morale in the garrisons was failing.

Valborga had returned from the breeding grounds, where she and her children had dealt with a band of red dragons that were hunting in areas claimed by the western dragons. Andrew was amazed to realize how territorial the giant dragons were; they had clearly marked hunting areas, and they were not about to let any other dragon hunt there.

Valborga's children had called her to lead the effort against the red dragons. They had surprised the hunting party late the preceding afternoon. Valborga confirmed Angus' observation that the red dragons were, in fact, faster than the great greens, but her blue-scales had no problem keeping up with them in both speed and maneuverability. In their brief battle, the green scales had flown on the outer perimeter of the red dragons, keeping them contained and preventing their escape. The blue scales flew inside the perimeter defined by the green scales.

Once contained by the green scales, the red dragons panicked.

One by one, the blue scales forced the red dragons to the ground. Once grounded, they perished quickly in the fire from the green scales.

Andrew was overwhelmed by the feeling of contempt that Valborga held for the red dragons. The western dragons were accustomed to battle, whether with man or nature. They took pride in skill and tactics.

The red dragons were trained in battle tactics, but their success depended on terrorizing their victims. When confronted by the western dragons, they were unable to develop a response; they broke formation, tried to flee, and ultimately died in the flames as they floundered about.

Angus and Andrew were encouraged by the report, but Andrew immediately asked the dragons if they could fly to the camp in the rear and help in the fight against the hundreds of red dragons they had seen launch earlier. The dogs turned and ran down the hill, transforming on the run and taking off at low level to stay below the ridgeline.

Climbing back on the boulder, Angus and Andrew again watched the garrisons as they consolidated into a single mass of humanity.

Even as they watched the scene below, both men worried about Charise and the others who had gathered to the West.

◆◆◆◆

Battle of the Dragons

Chapter the Eighteenth

About a half day's walk west of where Andrew and Angus fretted over Charise's fate, the people who had gathered were up with the sun and going about their business. Charise was moving about, Addiena at her feet, checking on everyone and making sure they were fed.

The call to arms had produced an amazing response. It was expected that the dragonslayers would respond quickly, but they were outnumbered three to one by their classmates who had chosen not to become dragonslayers. Charise mentioned her surprise at the number of non-dragonslayers that had arrived to Ian; his explanation brought tears to her eyes.

"More of them survive," he observed absently. "They haven't been to the meadow of the sword."

Seeing her response, he added, "Your Andrew has changed that, now. Maybe there will be more dragonslayers at our next reunion."

As Charise turned to leave, she looked to the East, where the sun was not well above the horizon. It took a moment before she could identify the red swarm that was coming at them with the sun to its back.

Addiena barked. Within seconds, every dog in the camp was barking, and the people were shifting about.

The dragonslayers and their classmates spread out, distributing themselves around the camp. The dogs ran to the outside edges of the camp, forming a ring at the extreme perimeter. The barking stopped abruptly, and every dog stood, silently watching the sky.

There was no battle plan. The campers had expected an attack by the eastern dragons, but they had no idea what form it would take or how many there would be. Everyone was watching the sky, waiting.

When the swarm was almost overhead, Charise looked about. Every man in sight was standing just as she was; sword in hand, eyes to the sky.

When the swarm arrived, the leaders broke right, flying in a circle around the camp. Charise realized what they were going to do; circle the camp, and then attack from all directions at once.

As the circle of darkness completed itself, Charise's sword hand rose instinctively.

When the first red dragon broke formation and dove toward the camp, the others began their attack. About twenty feet off the ground, the dragon belched flames at the man who was standing in front of it.

Quickly, the man stepped aside. The dragon never realized what had happened; by the time it could have known that the man was not inside the flames, the dragonslayer's sword had severed its neck. The dragon's head landed several feet away from where its body crashed to the ground.

Elsewhere around the camp, the scene was repeating itself. Dragons were attacking, and those that found an intended victim were discovering, too late, that the people on the ground were not terrified--they were prepared.

The dogs stood in their ring around the camp, watching the attack. When the last ranks of the airborne dragons began their attack, the dogs morphed into dragons and took to the sky.

Initially, the western dragons flew away from the camp in all directions. Anyone watching the flight would have concluded they were leaving; indeed, the eastern dragons that had seen the appearance of the great dragons watched them fly away from the camp, and then turned their attention back to the battle on the ground.

The great greens and blues initially flew close to the ground, well under the flight patterns of the eastern dragons. As they reached the outer limits of the dragons above them, the great greens climbed sharply, turning into a counter-clockwise flight patterns when they were above and behind the eastern horde.

When the greens were established around the eastern dragons, the blues turned up and into the mass of dragons above. Each blue picked a single red dragon as a target, and then closed on it like a jet fighter.

The eastern dragons were taken by surprise. The first attack of blue scales came from below and behind, and many of the eastern dragons never saw them before bursting into flames. After their initial pass, the blues continued to climb until they were above the mass of eastern dragons. As the blue scales reached an altitude above the red dragons, they performed a hammerhead turn and rolled gracefully into a dive, selecting their next target.

Initially, the red dragons were easy targets. They were in formation, focused on their inward and downward flight. The blues simply flew above or below them, then closed from behind.

Within minutes, the battle changed. The red dragons were not faring well on the ground. Dragon carcasses were piling up, and the dragonslayers had not lost a single fighter. As the red dragons saw their comrades lose their heads at the hands of the humans, they increasingly chose to fly over the camp instead of flying to the ground.

Things were not going well in the sky, either. The red dragons had realized what the blue scales were doing and had broken ranks, trying to escape the persistent fatal passes from below and above. Not a single red dragon had engaged the attacking blue scales; they fled, and the blues were fast enough to catch them on the run.

As chaos prevailed, red dragons began to flee, only to discover that the great greens blocked the sky in every direction. The larger green dragons were not fast enough to pursue the red dragons, but their fire was lethal if the red dragons flew into range.

And the circle of green scales was closing. With each pass, the green dragons closed their circle slightly, forcing the red dragons into tighter and tighter formation. Forced to fly in closer proximity to other dragons, the advantage of speed and maneuverability disappeared.

The blue scales no longer had targets moving in one direction; the red dragons were totally disorganized and flying in every direction. One by one, the blue scales gathered above the mass of red dragons. As they gathered, they began a clockwise flight pattern, moving in opposition to the direction of flight by the greens. The top layer of red dragons became the target, and the blues simply circled in a descending pattern, blasting fire on any dragon that flew into range.

The battle on the ground was expanding. Dragonslayers were moving outside the perimeter of the camp, spreading out to find open ground. The clutter of carcasses inside the camp was beginning to restrict the movements of the dragonslayers.

The red dragons faced death in every direction. Those that flew too close to the circling green dragons died in the fire. Those that landed died at the sword. The blue scales persistently lowered their flight path, forcing the red dragons lower and lower.

Inside the camp, Charise was literally jumping from carcass to carcass, dodging the fire of attacking dragons and adding to the carnage in the same manner as the dragonslayers around her. She sensed the loss of pattern in the attacks; the dragons were now being forced downward and they had no room to develop either speed or direction. The red dragons had initially been dive bombers, arriving with speed and carefully timed blasts of fire. Now there was a great flapping of wings and a reluctance to come within range of the deadly swords.

As the cyclone of green dragons drew tighter and tighter, the blue scales flew lower and lower. The sky was filled with flames as the crowd of red dragons forced some too close to the edge or too high in the crowd and the unfortunates were consumed in fire.

After a half hour of circling dragons and deadly swords, Charise realized that they were just slaughtering the red dragons. The attackers were no longer even belching flames; they were focusing their energies entirely on escape. When the red dragons reached the bottom, sides or top of the herd, others were pushing them toward danger, using their comrades as shields from the fire or swords. The bodies were piling up on the ground, and the ashes filled the air. But no matter what they did, the dragons eventually reached the bottom, top or sides of the melee and met their fate.

Erin and Valborga had met five red dragons on their trip to the west; five that thought they had escaped only to die in the flames on their way back to the east. When the two dragons arrived at the fight, it was nearly finished. The westerly wind carried the smell and ashes of burnt flesh, and the circle above the camp was tight around the edges and at the top. The two giant dragons circled outside the fight, watching for any escapees, but none came.

Finally, the green scales broke formation and move up and away from the center of the fight. On cue, the blue scales began again to dive through the red dragons, belching fire and scattering the remaining red dragons. As the tightly clustered dragons found gaps, they shot away from the fight only to encounter the green scales waiting just beyond.

None of the red dragons escaped.

When the fight was over, carnage was everywhere. Everyone on the ground had found bandanas or scarves to cover their mouth and noses, keeping out the rancid smoke and ash from the burning dragons. All were covered with blood and black soot, but all were standing.

The noncombatants began to emerge from under the wagons where they had taken shelter. Charise stumbled through the carcasses on the ground, joined by Ian as they surveyed the destruction. As the adrenaline of the fight began to subside, many of the combatants vomited, overwhelmed by the stench and blood.

As they moved through the carcasses, Ian and Charise told everyone to move to the open field where the green scale and blue scale dragons had landed. Soon, everyone was out of the main camp and had found their families and traveling companions. Two men were initially feared lost, but they eventually made it out of the camp and joined the rest of the troupe.

Ian surveyed the camp and turned to Charise.

"What a mess!" he observed. "How are we ever going to clear the bodies and clean up the camp?"

Addiena, Erin and Valborga joined them, still in their dragon form.

"If we can clear a path, we can move the wagons out," Charise observed. "But we can't leave these bodies lying about. They were nasty enough when they were alive, but the stench is horrible now that they are dead."

Erin walked away to confer with the other dragons. Soon, she returned.

In the soft whine of dragon speech, Erin explained that the dragons would move the bodies and clear a path for the humans to leave. Once the humans were out of the camp, the dragons could pile the bodies and burn them. Even the dragons were disgusted by the smell, but they were able to move the bodies which were far too heavy for the humans to wrestle with.

Charise nodded.

The dragons moved into the camp, throwing bodies and severed heads into piles. Soon there was room for the wagons to move, and the humans began to lead their teams and mounts out of the carnage, pulling wagons and carts behind them.

The sun was almost on the western horizon by the time the humans were clear and all of their belongings had been collected. Everyone was tired from the long day, but they all wanted to keep moving east, away from the battlefield.

Charise sent Erin and Valborga back to Andrew and Angus with news of the battle. Addiena had taken her dog form and stood with Charise. The rest of the dragons were working to clear the field and prepare the piles of bodies to be burned.

The humans finished preparing for the trek eastward. Charise and Ian led the way, followed by a long line of wagons, carts, and riders on horseback. Behind them, the first piles were being surrounded by dragons and burned to ash. Fortunately, the wind had shifted to the south, and the smoke and ash was not following the campers who were headed east.

At sundown, the travelers reached a river which ran from northeast to southwest. They would need to find a shallow, solid area to cross it, and the travelers were exhausted. The river presented an opportunity to wash off the blood and soot.

It was well after dark before everyone had a chance to clean up and prepare to rest. Ian established a guard schedule and posted them around the loosely assembled wagon train. Charise had sent Addiena east to verify that the soldiers were not on the move; she had returned with news that they were still encamped on the eastern slopes.

Everyone, except the guards, was ready to sleep off the exhaustion of the day. As more and more of the travelers found their sleeping bags or blankets, Ian returned to Charise.

"I'm going to ride to Andrew and Angus," he announced. "You can bring the rest of the troupe tomorrow. Do you know a good spot to set up camp between here and the soldiers?"

Charise nodded. "There is a large meadow about halfway through the foothills," she told the dragonslayer. "We can camp there, set up the forges and graze the horses and livestock. We can probably reach it tomorrow, if we can find a place to ford the river early in the morning. Hopefully, the battle will not start for at least a couple of days."

"I don't know how long we have," Ian observed, "but that's outside our control, so let's go ahead with your plan."

Charise reached up and kissed the dragonslayer on the cheek.

"Be careful," she said affectionately.

"I'll take Augustine," he said. "I don't think we need to worry about any more red dragons, but sometimes discretion is the better part of valor. I'll be OK," he concluded, mounting his horse.

Charise walked through the camp before lying down for the night. She spoke with the few who were still awake, telling them of the plans for the morrow. Spirits were high, even though most were exhausted.

When she finished her rounds, Charise lay alone in her blanket, worrying about her son and Angus. As she looked up, she saw a million stars and a full moon lighting the night. Remembering Angus' discussions about the uselessness of wasting energy on worry, her face shifted to an exhausted smile and she drifted off to sleep.

Ian arrived at the crest of the pass just before the dew began to settle, anticipating the dawn. Andrew lay on the overlook boulder; Angus slept in its shadow. Ian climbed up and crawled next to Andrew, looking out at the massed armies below.

"They do not yet seem ready to move," Andrew observed. "I think they are still waiting for the dragons to return." Smiling at the other dragonslayer, he noted, "Thanks to you and the others, they will be disappointed."

Ian nodded. After a while, he noted, "The dragons were wonderful. They came up with a plan on their own and executed it perfectly." His tone reflected pure admiration for his former adversaries.

Andrew's smile was visible in the light of the full moon. "Don't forget they have magic," he reminded his companion. "What one dragon knows, they all seem to know. Directing a battle with that kind of communication has to be much easier."

"Yes," Ian agreed. "But it was still impressive."

The two lay silently until the moon was waning and the first rays of light began to show over the horizon. As the light grew stronger, preparing for sunup, Angus appeared. The two younger dragonslayers moved over to make room for the Elder.

As the sun came up and the men in the garrisons below began to move about, Angus observed, "Do they seem to be moving slower today?"

Andrew watched for several minutes before responding.

"I think so," he finally agreed. "What do you think that means?"

"I'm not sure," Angus replied. "But it's probably not bad for us."

The two younger dragonslayers nodded in agreement. The threesome returned their attention to the garrisons, each trying to find something of value in the movements below.

As the dew burned off the grass, there was a gathering of several men in a tent that was centrally located among the men. From their vantage point, the dragonslayers could see that five of the men wore uniforms with bright plumage. Each man was accompanied by at least one other soldier, and by a dragon with its handler. The staff officers and dragon handlers waited outside as the brightly dressed men entered the tent.

"Generals?" Andrew asked the other two.

All agreed. It was a meeting of the generals.

"Well, Lads," the Elder observed, stretching his arms to either side. "Soon, we may get to do something besides lay on this rock."

Both young men laughed.

The generals all emerged from the tent together. The dragon-slayers could clearly see the generals barking orders to the staff offi-cers, who ran in all directions. Soon, ten horses were brought to the gathering area, and the officers all mounted steeds. As they moved forward on their horses, the staff officers raced forward, each carrying the colors and crest of their respective army. The dragon handlers fell in well behind, trotting along to keep up with the mounted officers.

As the horsemen moved westerly up the slope, Angus looked at Ian and Andrew. "Looks like they want a meeting, Lads," he observed. "Shall we accommodate them, or should we just send the dragons?"

The younger dragonslayers laughed. "I don't think it would be polite to send the dragons out," Andrew replied. "But it wouldn't hurt to take them along."

Angus, Ian and Andrew slid off the rock. Erin and Valborga sat, waiting with Ian's dragon, Augustine. The dragonslayers brushed the dust off their armor and set out down the slope, each with a dog trotting to his right side.

◆◆◆◆

Armies of the East

Chapter the Nineteenth

The three dragonslayers were strolling as they headed down the slopes. Angus was in the middle, with Andrew to his right and Ian to his left. Each dragonslayer's dragon was to his right, in their dog form. They walked through the open meadows, directly toward the approaching officers.

When the two parties were within ten feet, the officers with the staffs and colors reined their horses to the left and passed through the generals, stopping behind the dragons and their handlers. The dragons and handlers moved forward, each standing to the left of his general.

"Can you understand us?" the general in the center asked.

"Aye," Angus replied. What he did not tell them was that the dragons understood and transferred the speech telepathically to their dragonslayer. When Angus spoke, Erin's magic allowed the generals to understand.

Suddenly, the third red dragon lunged forward as if to attack. None of the dragonslayers or dogs moved.

"Hold your dragon!" the general barked. Looking appropriately chastised, the handler made a show of tightening his grip.

"I see your troops," Angus ventured. "Of course, you wanted us to see them or you would have massed them elsewhere."

The third general nodded.

"We would like to minimize the bloodshed," the general explained. "If you see how outnumbered you are, we hoped we could negotiate a peaceful surrender."

"We don't require surrender," Angus replied flatly. "You can just leave us alone and none will be necessary."

All five generals laughed. The general in the center leaned forward on his right arm as if to move closer to Angus.

"We have two hundred thousand soldiers and as many dragons. If we have to fight our way through the pass, they will be in no mood for mercy," he said ominously.

"I think you may be a bit short on the dragons," Angus replied lightly. "The ones you sent out yesterday won't be coming back." After a brief pause, he added, "And your soldiers who ventured to the west side of the pass are gone as well."

The second general sat high in his saddle. "There's a great difference between a small scouting party and an attack by two hundred thousand battle-hardened troops!" He seemed indignant that Angus would treat their threat so lightly.

"Aye," Angus agreed. "There are more funeral pyres when we face an army."

As Angus verbally sparred with the generals, Andrew's attention shifted from the general to general. In the corner of his eye, he could see the fourth dragon handler feeding the leash through his hand, creating a long stretch of slack and releasing his grip on the rope.

"The dragon's going to attack you," he said mentally to Valborga. "Don't move."

Valborga sat on her haunches to let Andrew know she heard.

As Angus began to say, "We are a peaceful people," the dragon lurched forward, mouth open, at Valborga.

The generals could not turn quickly enough to see Andrew's right hand, thumb up, reach across and grab the hilt of his sword. He was holding it in a reverse grip, blade down. They were, however, all watching by the time Andrew took two quick steps to the right as the sword leapt from his scabbard, swinging horizontally. When the hilt guard touched the dragon's neck, the blade swung counterclockwise and upward, severing the dragon's neck from the bottom up.

The dragon's head fell away and its body tumbled to the ground next to Andrew as the sword turned upright. Releasing the hilt, Andrew turned his hand and caught it while it was suspended in mid-air. Dropping the blade flat into the grass, he wiped the dragon's blood from his sword, leaving a red "X" on the grass in front of him.

Andrew returned his sword to its scabbard and stepped back into his place next to Angus.

"We have no desire to do battle with you or your armies. We have not enjoyed the slaughter of your dragons," Angus continued, uninterrupted by Andrew and the dragon. He had not even glanced Andrew's direction, and there was no change in his speech pattern. It was as if he were totally unaware of the events to his immediate right.

"As a matter of fact," he continued, "we're not even sure why you would want to attack us. There are no estates to plunder, no hoards of gold to be gained. We are a simple people, and the only nobility is

Prince Andrew here." Angus motioned to his right. "And I believe he carries everything he owns on his back."

Andrew bowed his head slightly, acknowledging Angus' introduction.

"We are familiar with battle, at least on an individual basis," Angus continued. "And we have only one rule--at the end of the battle, there is only one combatant standing. So, if you choose to attack, just realize that you will either have to slaughter each and every one of us..." The old dragonslayer paused for effect.

"Or be killed. Either way, it will be over when it is over."

The generals sat on their mounts, looking at the dragonslayers in front of them. Angus had no doubt that Garand had told these men about the significance of armor color--blue, then green. They were facing one set of green armor, two turquoise. Angus was counting on their understanding--and appreciation--of what it took to earn those colors.

"Then..." interjected the general in the middle, "we will prepare our troops, and you will prepare yours."

"We will see you on the field of valor, then," Angus said. Pointing behind him, he added, "Which will be right there where the rocks narrow. That is where we will make our stand."

With a quick bow of his head, Angus ended the meeting. He turned on his heel and headed back up the hill. Ian and Andrew turned a split second later and walked one step behind. The three dogs held their position, sitting on their haunches and watching the generals.

As the generals turned their horses to leave, the three dogs morphed into their dragon forms and launched into the sky. The horses spooked, and one threw its general unceremoniously to the ground. The general's aide jumped off his mount as soon as it stopped bucking, running to help the general.

Erin, Valborga, and Augustine went airborne with three pushes with their huge wings, and then glided effortlessly down the hillside toward the troops. Flying at low level and high speed, they made lazy loops over the soldiers and dragons, giving them a good view of the size of three great green dragons. As they turned sharply back up the ridge, the sun reflected off their brilliant scales as if from a mirror.

Back in formation, the three great greens passed swiftly over the three humans walking up the hill, casting great shadows over them as they walked. The three men looked up and waived to their dragons.

As the dragons reached the narrow point of the pass, they landed and morphed back into dogs. Each turned and lay on the ground, waiting for his or her dragonslayer.

By the time the dragonslayers were speaking to the generals, Charise and her fellow travelers had broken camp and found a place to ford the river. They moved quickly to the east, through the foothills toward the meadow where they would make their battle camp.

It was lunch time when the wagon train arrived at the meadow in the foothills. Charise gathered the travelers together and, over lunch, they all discussed the best way to organize and be prepared for the work ahead.

"Do not forget," Charise warned, "that there is no guarantee that we will be successful in holding back the troops. We can assume their numbers will be greatly reduced, even if they succeed. Each of us needs to plan, now, how we will break camp and how we will flee if the battle goes poorly."

Everyone nodded their agreement.

After lunch, the wagons were positioned in a manner that would allow the camp to be broken quickly if needed. After some discussion, those with livestock decided that they would simply abandon them in the meadow if they had to leave. For the moment, they would allow the stock open grazing, with several men assigned to keep the herd from wandering off into the forest surrounding the meadow.

Forges were offloaded, and the blacksmiths went into the forest to harvest wood for their fires. The butcher slaughtered one pig and one young bull, preparing the meat for the crowd. Cooks set up tents and makeshift tables to provide cover and seating.

By dark, the camp was ready to sustain the troops and their equipment. Guard schedules were worked out, and everyone had something to do as they waited for the battle.

Conroy, a dragonslayer, left right after lunch with food, water and other provisions for the men at the ridge. It was early afternoon when he arrived, and the four dragonslayers ate in plain view of the men in the meadow below. Andrew told Conroy of the meeting with the generals, and they all discussed the tactics that would be needed when the attack came.

The dragonslayers had agreed that they should be as obvious as possible, letting the troops below see them going about their normal activities. While the actual numbers of dragons and troops would not be shown until the battle, they believed the more they demonstrated a lack of concern, the better.

The dragons flew away from camp to hunt for food. They made their departure in full view of the soldiers below, heading east before breaking north to hunt in the forests surrounding the camp below.

Conroy returned to camp in the early evening, sharing the day's events with the travelers at the camp. Andrew had decided that approximately one third of the combatants should move to the pass, prepared to respond quickly to an attack. Each day, they would be replaced and return to the rear camp where there was plenty of provisions and they could rest. By rotating one day forward, two days in the rear, he hoped to keep everyone rested and fed as well as possible while they waited for the attack.

Conroy led the first group of combatants to the east just before dark. There was a full moon and clear skies, so they could travel in the early hours of the night by the light of the moon. The group of about two hundred dragonslayers and their classmates found places to sleep close to the pass, lying in full armor and prepared to respond quickly if needed.

Angus, Ian, and Andrew took turns lying on the boulder and watching the camps below. There was considerable movement in two of the camps, but the other three armies seemed to be quiet. The dragonslayers discussed the activity, but could not reach any conclusion about what it might mean.

As day broke, the two camps that had been active in the night began to break camp. Andrew reported the movement to the combatants, and they all prepared for battle.

By mid-day, the camps were fully broken, wagons and pack animals loaded and horses saddled. At the pass, everyone was in place for the first wave of the attack.

Andrew was the lookout when the soldiers started moving out. He called for Angus, who joined him immediately.

The armies were heading east, away from the ridge.

"Where do you think they are going?" Andrew asked the old dragonslayer.

"I have no idea," Angus responded. "Are we sure there are no other passes where they could cross to the West?"

Andrew slid off his perch and called for Erin and Valborga. Within a moment, both dragons arrived in their dog form.

A brief consultation with the dragons confirmed that this was the only location where a crossing could be made. Erin knew of another pass well to the south, but it was much higher and more difficult crossing and it would be winter before the soldiers could relocate and gather there.

The second group of combatants arrived in the early afternoon, and the first cohort remained on the pass until almost dark. Finally, the first cohort left for camp, and the second settled in for the evening.

As first light arrived, there was a flurry of activity in the remaining camps. Like the first two armies, camp was broken and the army was ready to move by mid-day. Again, the combatants on the ridge prepared for an attack.

One by one, the armies left to the east. By the time the third cohort of dragonslayers arrived at the ridge, the last army was moving out.

"Do you think they are giving up?" Andrew asked Angus.

"I don't know," the old dragonslayer responded. "I can't see where they could be setting a trap."

Looking over the edge of the boulder at Erin, Angus asked her if she would fly over the armies and verify their direction of travel. Within minutes, Erin, Valborga, and Augustine were airborne, flying above the few afternoon clouds that had gathered to the east.

The second cohort waited with their replacements for news from the dragons. Hope ran high that the armies were leaving, but no one dared become too optimistic until they were sure.

At sundown, the three dragons landed just below the crest of the pass and morphed into their dog forms. Minutes later, they reported back to their dragonslayers.

The armies were moving east, then northeast.

They were going home.

A cheer arose from the combatants as the news traveled quickly through the camp. Men were hugging each other, and the sound of victory was in the air.

Two dragons were dispatched to the camp in the rear to carry the news.

The combatants would wait another day, just to be sure this was not a trick. Dragons were dispatched to keep track of the armies. The second cohort decided to remain at the ridge, celebrating with their comrades.

It was dark when Charise arrived at the ridge. Four hundred men parted to let her pass through the crowd to the boulder where her son and Angus were still stationed. She was crying as she hugged her son, and more tears flowed when she wrapped her arms around the old dragonslayer.

With knowing smiles, the men turned away to avoid staring at the beautiful woman who was showering their teacher with kisses.

Everyone on the ridge was too excited to sleep. Every couple of hours, dragons returned with word of the armies--they were all still moving away, traveling through the night.

At daybreak, the entire troupe mounted their horses and headed west.

The second war of the dragons had ended and the provinces were again safe. There would be no more battles this year. As they rode, the men told each other stories of the battle of the dragons, and legends were constructed to tell around campfires for years to come.

High above, dragons flew in lazy eights, enjoying the day.

The riders had formed up behind Andrew, Angus, and Charise, who rode in the lead.

"You have proven your metal, Lad," Angus commented to Andrew as they rode.

Andrew laughed. "We weren't even there for the battle of the dragons," he said. "Mom and the others are the heroes."

Angus smiled. "There would have been no green or blue scale dragons at the battle if you had not changed the rules of engagement at the meadow of the sword. And, without our own dragons, the outcome might have been very different."

Andrew fell silent, clearly embarrassed by the compliments from his teacher.

As they rode into camp, the others ran out to join them.

Celebrations lasted late into the night. News of the retreat by the armies had traveled quickly, and people from the nearer towns and farms had raced out to join the campers. As the mead flowed and people danced around the fire, Angus sat with Charise at the edge of the camp and watched the celebration.

"I have to admit," Charise said quietly, "living with you is never boring."

Angus laughed.

"Aye," he agreed. "When I was exiled to the world of science, I never dreamed I would meet someone like you, or Andrew, or Latisha."

Turning to Charise, he held her face in his hands and kissed her, full on the lips. Charise nearly fell off her seat from surprise; it was the first time the old dragonslayer had ever initiated such contact.

"It has been good," the old dragonslayer said as he released her and settled back.

"Very good," Charise agreed, laying her head on his shoulder and clutching his arm tightly.

◆◆◆◆

Dragon Claws

Chapter the Last

Tales of the second dragon wars were just beginning to be elaborated when Andrew and Latisha kissed their mother goodbye and rode off to the South. Ian, still smitten by Latisha, rode with them.

Latisha rode between the men, Ian to her left and Andrew to her right. To the right of Andrew's horse trotted Valborga, the dragon, in her dog form. To the left of Ian, the dragon Augustine kept pace with the horses, also in his dog form.

Charise watched her offspring ride out of sight, then set about breaking camp. The old dragonslayer, Angus, puttered about domestically, clearing dishes and folding blankets to help Charise with the final chores.

Charise stopped mid-stride, looking to the South as she absently folded her blanket.

"Do you think they'll be OK?" she asked the old dragonslayer, absently.

"They'll be fine," he replied merrily. "I can't imagine a challenge two dragonslayers and a sorceress could not handle."

Her smile was fleeting, but Charise turned her attention back to packing and loading the camp. Within the hour, she was done.

As the threesome rode south, the northern forest gave way to southern palm.

"Did you do that?" Andrew asked his sister.

"Yeah," she said absently. "I got tired of the cold weather."

"Are we still in the same time zone?"

Latisha smiled. "No," she said coyly.

"Are we at least in the same dimension?" Andrew insisted.

"Yes," his sister laughed. "We're still in the land of dragons."

Sensing the change of regions, Augustine and Valborga morphed into their dragon form, taking to the sky in search of suitable food.

"Where are we going?" Ian asked absently.

Both Andrew and Latisha looked at him and laughed.

"Yes," Andrew asked his sister in a teasing voice. "Where *are* we going?"

"South," she replied simply. "Beyond that, I have no definite plans."

The men simultaneously gave indifferent shrugs.

As dark descended, the threesome made a camp near an over-cropping of rock which looked out over a sizeable meadow. The site offered cover in the event of rain, as well as plenty of loose wood for a fire. Ian gathered wood while Andrew and Latisha made camp.

"You're adjusting well," Latisha commented to her brother, "for a city kid."

Andrew laughed. "I think necessity is the mother, if you know what I mean. There wasn't really any time to worry about coming

196

to the land of dragons—it just happened. From there on, I've been a little busy."

Latisha smiled.

"Maybe we can stay here a few days," she suggested. "There is much you can learn from Ian, and it's probably a good idea for you to learn a little more about wilderness camping before we get too far along on our trip."

Ian returned as Andrew and Latisha were finishing their conversation. Latisha quickly recapped their conversation. Ian looked slightly confused about her suggestion that he train Andrew.

"I've seen him battle a dragon," he said to Latisha. Turning to Andrew, he added, "I don't think there's much I can teach you about that sword that you don't already know."

"I think Latisha and Angus took care of training me with the sword," Andrew agreed. He had never asked his sister about the video game "Dragon Tails", but he had come to suspect she had something to do with the game and the powers he had acquired playing it.

Latisha nodded. "Yes," she admitted, "I did create Dragon Tails. But there is much, much more for you to learn besides how to slay a dragon." Pointing to the wood stacked next to the fire pit Ian had quickly assembled, she said simply, "Like building a fire."

Both men nodded. Ian walked over to the fire pit, followed closely by Andrew.

"Start with some kindling," he explained as he gathered small twigs and grass.

Latisha ignored them as she put together a quick dinner with jerky, fruit and vegetables they had brought from the battle encampment.

The next several days were relatively uneventful as Ian and Latisha taught Andrew about living without the modern conveniences he had always enjoyed. On the second day, Andrew made an unfortunate choice of leaves when he toileted and Latisha had to make a salve to reduce the irritation on his bottom. Otherwise, he learned quickly and without significant pain.

On the fifth morning, the trio broke camp and again rode south. The dragons were flying above, preferring their full dragon form to their dog shapes.

At mid-day, a fork in the road led either South or East. Without discussion, they all headed south along the right fork. Within minutes, Latisha reined in her horse. Andrew and Ian followed suit, looking at the young woman and waiting for an explanation.

After a moment, Latisha said, "I think we needed the other fork."

"East?" Ian asked.

"East," Latisha confirmed.

Without discussion, the men turned their horses and headed back up the road. As they passed, Latisha turned her horse and joined them.

Overhead, the dragons flew in Lazy-8's, unconcerned with the change in direction.

Within an hour, they turned a bend and encountered a young woman sitting on a draught horse. She was clearly oriental, dressed in traditional work garb and looking toward them as they approached.

The three rode within a few feet of the young woman, who had not moved. At first, Andrew could not figure out what was different about her—he looked again and again, almost staring, because there was something unique and he couldn't quite place it. When they stopped before her, he realized what it was—she was blind!

The riders waited for the young woman to speak. Finally, she spoke in a language Andrew recognized as Vietnamese from its sing-song qualities. He missed the first few words, and then began to understand her. Looking at his sister, her nod confirmed that she was translating telepathically.

Her name was D'ao. The sound rolled so beautifully off her lips, and Andrew could smell orange blossoms from just thinking about it. D'ao had sensed them as they rode south and believed they would find her if she stopped. Andrew listened to her and felt himself being drawn to her in an extraordinary way.

"Andrew!" he heard his sister say. Looking to her, he could see the scolding look he knew so well from living with their mother.

Shaking off his infatuation with the stranger, Andrew listened to her simple request to join them on their journey south.

"That would be wonderful," Latisha volunteered without consulting the men.

The three again reversed directions, heading back along the road in a westerly direction until reaching the road which led north-south. Latisha and Ian rode in the front, while Andrew followed alongside D'ao. Andrew's horse seemed almost tiny next to D'ao's draught horse, but the larger horse had no problem keeping pace with the smaller mounts.

After riding south until nearly sunset, they came upon some caves that offered protection for the night. Ian took Andrew to show him how to snare rabbits, while Latisha and D'ao set camp. By nightfall, dinner was ready and the four travelers sat around the fire dining on rabbit, green beans and potatoes.

"D'ao," Latisha ventured between bites, "how did you become blind?" Both men looked at her, shocked by her direct question. Latisha ignored them.

"I was born blind," D'ao responded softly. "My family kept me until I was three, when the famine came and was killing the children and old people. They took me to a monastery, where the monks took me in. They taught me to use my remaining senses, and to trust my instincts."

"Where are you going?" Andrew ventured, wanting to be included in the conversation.

"South, where the bitter beans grow," she replied proudly. "There I will buy beans and a cart, and I will take a load of the beans to my fathers. They grind them and mix them with sugar and milk to make a wonderful drink."

Latisha drew in a deep breath through her nose, simulating the act of smelling something wonderful. "Chocolate," she said reverently.

D'ao smiled affectionately. "I can smell it in your mind. It is wonderful."

"How do you find your way?" Ian ventured.

"Sun on the back of my head in the morning," D'ao responded simply, "sun in my face after lunch. If the road splits, I keep the sun in the right position and I work my way south and west."

Ian nodded approvingly. After a moment, his face took on a look of curiosity. "How do you stay on the road?" he asked.

"The horse likes the road," she smiled. "Unless I force him off it, he follows it without any help from me."

Ian nodded, satisfied with the answer. Everyone ate silently until D'ao laid her rabbit leg down and ventured, "I sense that the magic is strong in each of you. You," she paused, looking toward Latisha, "puzzle me. Your soul and magic feel as if they are worn very smooth, yet your physical presence feels young."

Latisha smiled. "That is true," Latisha confirmed. "This is one of many, many lifetimes for me."

D'ao tipped her head curiously. "Really?" she asked. "Are you approaching nirvana?"

"No," Latisha replied frankly, "nirvana is not my goal. I try to learn and improve with each incarnation, but I do not seek nirvana."

D'ao seemed satisfied. After a moment, she turned to Ian. "Your magic is very strong, but not as strong as theirs. You feel as if you've known much violence..." Her voice trailed off at the end of her statement. Turning as if to look behind her, she said in a delighted voice, "Dragons!"

Within a moment, Augustine and Valborga joined the camp in their dog forms. As D'ao reached out and Valborga stuck her head in the newcomer's hand, her face showed her puzzlement.

"They take dog form," Latisha volunteered, "when they are with us. It makes it easier for them to move around, and more comfortable for us as well."

D'ao laughed in delight as the dogs pushed each other away from her hands, each demanding her attention in turn.

Andrew looked down and his heart was gone. Every fiber in his body told him there would never be another woman like this one. The raw courage it took for a blind woman to travel from the Far East to Africa in search of cocoa beans was unimaginable to him. But the clincher was the pure joy she displayed with the dragons; she was so like a little girl, yet she was clearly a woman.

Ian finally got the chance to explain that he had been a dragonslayer, and D'ao's face showed her shock and concern. As he explained why there had been dragon slaying, and that Andrew had found a way to change that, she seemed impressed.

The foursome chatted away the evening until the fire was smoldering embers. As Latisha stood and began preparing for bed, D'ao looked at Andrew and said, "The road has been long and cold. May I lay with you tonight?"

Andrew was shocked, but overjoyed. He nodded, forgetting for the moment that D'ao was blind.

D'ao smiled. "I take that as a yes," she said as if she could see Andrew's head bobbing.

After the blankets were laid, Latisha and D'ao went into the shrubs first, and then the men took their turns. When Andrew came back, he nearly ran over Latisha, who was standing in the shadow of a giant oak just outside the main camp. The light from the fire glowed behind the tree, but they were fully hidden by its shadow.

"If you don't treat her like the angel she is," Latisha warned her brother, "I will turn you into a frog!"

Andrew was startled. "Can you do that?" he asked.

"No," Latisha admitted, "but I can do things that are far worse. I just haven't thought of the right one yet. But, it will be horrible..." she warned, shaking her finger in his face.

Andrew laughed at his sister. "I think she's an angel, too," he told her softly. "And I think I'm getting the hang of this telepathy thing. I could see, or feel, or... whatever, what she meant by 'lay with me'. I'll be a gentleman," he reassured her.

As Andrew cuddled with D'ao, lying against her back with his arm over her, he had the definite feeling that this was what heaven would be like. As if she had read his thoughts, D'ao scooted back to close the already narrow gap between their bodies.

Andrew awoke with an incredible sense of well-being. The sky seemed bluer, he had rested well, and the day was full of promise. If this is what being married felt like, he was going to have to change his opinion and get married! Preferably, he thought, to D'ao.

Within an hour after sunrise, the foursome had eaten, broken camp, and saddled their mounts. Once the fire was cold, they resumed their journey south. Conversation was light, and Andrew felt free to look closely at D'ao's face as they travelled along. She was radiantly beautiful, and he felt a tug at his heart each time he returned his gaze to her eyes, which stared off into the distance.

At mid-day, Andrew was gazing at D'ao when she suddenly became intensely focused ahead. Without warning, she spurred her horse forward and slipped into the gap between Latisha and Ian. The dragons had been flying above, but Andrew heard the thundering of their dog feet as they ran to catch up with the horses.

Andrew's hair stood up on the back of his neck.

D'ao chattered at Latisha, but Andrew couldn't hear enough to make out what she was saying.

Without warning, the three front riders stopped and Andrew eased forward to join their line, pushing between Latisha and D'ao. Augustine and Valborga stood next to the riders, ready for trouble but patiently waiting their turn.

Three men stood in the road ahead of them. Their position, as well as the weapons in their hands, indicated that they were ready for trouble.

Andrew was hardly worried. He was a dragonslayer, and these men presented very little threat to him or to Ian. He wasn't sure about Latisha, but he sensed she was probably more dangerous than either of the men.

D'ao handed him the reins of her horse. Before he realized it, D'ao was off her horse and he was holding its reins while she moved ahead of her fellow travelers.

Andrew was about to fasten the reins of D'ao's horse to the saddle horn on his mount when Latisha looked at him and said sternly, "Hold her horse."

Andrew's temper flared. "No," he said. "She has no business facing those men. I'm not going to sit her while she gets hurt or worse!"

Latisha reached over and put her hand over his, pushing it down against his saddle with a surprising amount of force.

"You're going to sit right there. These men are after her, and she chooses to deal with them on her own terms. Do NOT disrespect her by interfering!"

D'ao stood, toe to toe, with a man clearly twice her size. He started off in a reasonable tone, but his anger showed quickly. He was insisting, and she was declining, but beyond that Andrew could not determine what the conversation was about.

Below his right foot, Valborga barked quietly. Andrew looked down, and then followed her gaze into the tree line to their right. He could see something moving there, slipping about among the bushes. There were men out there, and Andrew began paying attention from the corner of his eye.

Slightly ahead of him, Latisha kicked her right foot over the saddle and slid off her mount. Turning, she walked behind him, turning her back to D'ao and the men in the road.

Andrew felt Ian tense and knew he was looking to the left. They were surrounded, and D'ao had the front, Latisha had the rear.

Andrew kicked his left leg over the saddle and slid to the ground. The movement in the bushes stopped, but he could feel them out there. He did not know how many there were, but he was sure there were several.

Without looking, he knew Ian had slipped off his horse and was watching to the left.

Andrew became increasingly nervous about the man speaking with D'ao. The volume was getting higher, and D'ao quietly insisted while the man became louder and louder. Andrew was splitting his attention between the verbal confrontation and the men in the woods, and he was getting increasingly nervous.

Two men flanked the belligerent one who was confronting D'ao, standing a few feet back. When the man to D'ao's right front pulled out his bow and began to string an arrow, Andrew drew both sword and long knife; he was ready to throw the knife if the man began to draw the arrow.

Andrew's reflexes were unnaturally fast since becoming a dragonslayer. Most people could not even see his hands move when he was reaching for his sword or knife. Yet, before he could even bring his knife up to throwing position, a chain snaked out from D'ao's right hand and the crescent-shaped knife at the end cut the bow and string, returning to her hand as quickly as it had reached out.

The man confronting D'ao stopped shouting, turning to look at the man standing with the bow in two pieces. He turned back to D'ao and raised his hand as if to strike her.

D'ao's right foot came straight up between her and the man, reaching upward until it was above his head. Her heel came down hard on his clavicle, and the sound of bones breaking was audible to everyone.

The man screamed.

The man to his right drew his sword. Andrew drew back his long knife just in time to see the chain snake out and the man's head was neatly severed by the crescent at its end.

Men began to run out of the woods from all directions. As Andrew prepared to defend himself and D'ao, he heard her say, "Dragons!"

In an instant, Augustine and Valborga morphed into their dragon forms. The men stopped, then turned and ran in panic.

In a second, Andrew was standing next to D'ao. The man who had been arguing with her was kneeling on the ground, holding his useless left arm.

D'ao knelt before the man, reaching out to his injured shoulder. When she touched his shoulder with her right hand, she reached with her left hand and touched the breastplate of Andrew's armor. Her right hand began to glow.

Andrew could see the healing as the shoulder aligned itself and the pain disappeared from the man's face.

"I am sorry for your loss," D'ao said quietly, looking at the remains of the man she had decapitated. "But you must not try to stop me on my quest. The gold coins that my fathers gave me are for the bitter beans, and I must guard them. If you try to stop me again, I am afraid that many will die."

Silently, the man nodded. He stood, then walked to the headless corpse and drew it up over his left shoulder. Taking the head by its hair in his right hand, he walked slowly away.

D'ao turned to Andrew.

"Thank you for not interfering," she said quietly; her tone was sincere. "If you had begun the fight, many would have died. I was hoping this would be a bloodless confrontation, but it was not meant to be."

Andrew shook his head. "I'm glad it turned out as well as it did."

Latisha and Ian had joined them.

Without a word, the foursome mounted and continued down the road to the South. Ian and Latisha were again in the lead, while Andrew and D'ao followed. They rode the rest of the day without a word, each member of the group lost in his or her own thoughts.

As the sun was setting, the foursome found an inn where they could get baths and beds. After cleaning up, they dined. Not a word was said by any of the travelers until they were settled in front of the fire, enjoying the local wine.

Finally, Andrew broke the silence by asking, "What was that weapon you used back there?"

"In Japan they call it Kusarigama—chain with blade," D'ao explained. "In China it is called Longxu hook --Dragon's Beard. This particular version is called Mong vuot cua con rong--Claws of the Dragon—in Vietnamese. The crescents are designed based on the shape of the claws of the red dragons of the east. They are not as large as the claws of the great greens, but you can see that they are quite effective."

"And how do you know where and when to throw them?" Andrew asked, amazed.

"I can feel the energy created by animals, including people," D'ao explained patiently. "It gives me the information I need to throw them accurately."

"Could you feel the bow in that man's hand?" Ian asked, incredulously.

"Is that what it was?" D'ao asked. "I could not tell what it was, but I could feel his aggression reaching a peak, so I threw in front of him hoping to disable whatever weapon he might have."

Andrew laughed. "That was brave," he commented.

"Not really," D'ao observed patiently. "I had the three of you right there, if things went badly," she explained. "I didn't want you to be involved, but I knew you were willing. I also knew the dragons were anxious to help, but I kept them in reserve until I believed they could end the confrontation."

Augustine and Valborga had been lying in front of the fire. Both dogs rose and walked to D'ao. She petted each of them, one with each hand, and each began rapid thumping of one back leg. Clearly, the loved the attention D'ao was giving them.

Andrew felt a slight pang of jealousy.

Without explanation, D'ao turned her face toward Andrew, curiosity showing clearly in her expression. Then she smiled.

Latisha laughed.

Ian looked totally confused.

Andrew saw the look on D'ao's face and needed no further explanation. She knew.

D'ao knew Andrew was in love with her.

Andrew was mortified. Without a word, he turned and went upstairs to the room he had hoped to share with D'ao. In his heart, he knew that was never going to happen now—she knew how he felt, and she would surely build a wall to keep him out. He would never have his chance to make her feel toward him the way he felt about her. Dejected, he sat on the side of the bed and put his head in his hands.

There was no sound, but he felt her presence, standing in front of him. Andrew looked up. D'ao was squatting in front of him, bringing her face to the same level as his. When he looked up, she took his face between her hands and leaned in.

The kiss was exquisite.

In the morning, Andrew and D'ao joined Ian and Latisha for breakfast. Latisha was so pleased she could barely contain herself.

"Well, brother," she said coyly, "have we made our peace?"

"Yes," he said. "I think we have."

When the foursome continued their journey to the south, Ian and Latisha rode closer than before—so close, their stirrups would occasionally touch.

Andrew and D'ao rode even closer.

◆◆◆◆

Post Script

As the two young couples continued south toward the land of the bitter beans, Charise and Angus were saying their good-byes at the door of her apartment.

"Are you sure you will be OK without Andrew and Latisha here?" the old dragonslayer asked.

"Yes," Charise said affectionately. "Are you sure you won't stay with me?"

"I should," Angus replied thoughtfully, "but there is still much to do in preparing the provinces for collective rule. I know not what I can do, but I know they need my help."

Charise leaned toward the old man and gave him a kiss on the lips.

"Of course," he said when they finished the kiss, "one more day wouldn't hurt."

Charise laughed. "That's what you've been saying for the last thirty days. Go, or stay. It's time to make up your mind."

Angus smiled.

"Keep my room for me?" he asked simply.

"Of course," Charise responded.

Angus turned and walked away with Erin.

Charise stood in the door, with Addiena at her feet, watching the old dragonslayer walk away with Addiena's daughter. When they were out of sight, she closed the door and began her day's chores.

In the land of dragons, a sword was drawn from the dirt which held it upright in a meadow. Looking at its legend, the sorcerer smiled and slipped it inside his robe.

The End Of One Great Adventure Is Almost Always The Beginning Of Another.

◆◆◆◆